The Crows

Also by Hermann Stehr from K A Nitz:

The Engraver

Meicke, the Devil

The Shingle Maker and Other Tales

Leonore Griebel

The Buried God

The Shimmer of the Assistant and Other Tales

The Twilight and Other Tales

Three Nights

Stories from the Mandel House

The Runaway Heart and Other Tales

The Crows

Hermann Stehr

K A Nitz

WELLINGTON

To dear Arthur Fundner,
for the 25th year of our friendship.

1

Hey, Manja, please come here," Professor Weitfeld said to his wife who was speaking excitedly with a lady from the balcony and so could not hear him. But even if she had stood there quite still, it would have been impossible for her to understand the intentionally muted voice of her husband. For that reason, the conversation of both women continued briskly.

"Yes, just think, Mrs Weitfeld," he heard the strong, not unpleasant, commanding voice of the lady standing below echoing up loudly, "just think of the luck of having gone forward thirty kilometres in three days and that on a front of 150 kilometres, a hundred and fifty kilometres."

"A hundred ...," his wife repeated in awe.

"Yes, a hundred and fifty kilometres — makes for fifteen hundred square kilometres of land won, seventy thousand prisoners, Soissons captured, the Vesle crossed, the Ardre, the Chemin des Dames ours in the rout, filled with munitions stores, transport depots, airfields. It's hard to take in, hard to comprehend! Well, and not the least, the downright enormous pile of provisions. Mountains of preserved food, flour, even chocolate. How would that suit the Professor's wife, a case of chocolate?"

"Oh, I beg, spare me, Mrs Forstmeister. Or else I'll have a bad day."

"I believe you. Me too. That is, I would have as well. If my Fritz weren't in the mess. Think of it!"

"So, your son is involved in it! How do you know exactly?"

"Well, of course! He is in the Crown Prince's army."

The Professor, who, standing by the other window, had been listening to the conversation, turned away with gloomy face and looked again through the treetops out into the countryside.

The conversation behind him continued passionately. Finally he could not endure it any longer and called out loudly and impatiently, "Manja, please, come here, please."

After that, he heard his wife say, "Forgive me, Mrs Forstmeister! My husband is calling me from the other room. So, I'll definitely come over to you this afternoon."

"But keep your word. Understand, dear! Give my greetings to your husband and tell him that my husband is certain it will all be over in eight weeks at the soonest."

"God yes, if it were only true!"

"Yes, if it were! This eternal bloodshed! No, you can hardly endure it anymore! So, farewell until this afternoon!"

"Farewell!"

The balcony door creaked shut and his wife came over to him, laid her hand on his shoulder and began talking passionately about the "splendid, unparalleled success of the Crown Prince's offensive". She indulged in hopes of peace and the future and talked more and more rashly of the fame and brilliance of Germany after the war, its rise in the world, its might and that it would be a royal delight to be a German. Weitfeld had listened without moving, and even now, when his wife had come to the end with a bitter trembling in her voice, he did not stir and answered with not a sound, but just continued to look out through the treetops into the fields, behind which the beautifully arranged high undulating wall of the Sudeten Mountains passed into the blueness.

"Well, what are you thinking then, husband?" she said testily. "You're like a well with a hand pump. Without putting effort in, you get nothing out."

"Look over there, please," he said softly.

"Where then? — At the lime trees?"

"No, further out into the fields, behind the stripes of grain."

"There? The meadow?"

"No, still a bit further behind the field. I mean the little hillock with which the field rises into the sky."

"Oh yes, beautiful. There are three little heaps of manure and on the middle one sits a crow."

"I meant simply that," Weitfeld said with a gently ironic smile. "You see, it turns sedately and points its head sometimes right, sometimes left and gathers its wings again and again. The hot air flitters around it and makes its image uncertain and trembling like a figment of your imagination. Do you see?"

"How couldn't I? But that isn't really very strange, if you ... but, please, don't put me off! No! It isn't strange at all. Absolutely not." His wife's face was flaring up with the redness of displeasure and she leant against the wall of the window niche. Weitfeld observed with large, calm eyes this attempt at insurrection, let a disapproving pause occur and then said with deliberate charitableness, "I ask you, Manja, to rein in your impatience even more than usual today. It is really about an important clarification in an important matter — also for the two of us. Do we not want to proceed calmly and thoroughly? You can then still add what you have to say against me."

"If you allow it. Right? Haha! — Well, good then. — What do you want to say?"

"Dear! I beg you. On a smouldering plain, no corn grows, said the Arab, and you can't think with a bitterly upset heart. Do you not want to listen to me with calm open-mindedness?"

"Oh, but look, now the crow is flying away and the three manure heaps are left alone. I think there is no point in the whole matter anymore. — — If you don't want to provoke the great debate today that you have talked about for so long."

The Professor let his left hand slowly glide down the window frame, clasped his hands together behind his back and strode thoughtfully into the room.

"Like the crow, just like the crow," he murmured softly.

"What did you say?" she asked from behind his back.

The Professor paused in the middle of the room and, turning to her, he said calmly, "I meant the crow. You see, Manja, when I spotted it before, saw it before, I had the feeling the bird had already been sitting an eternity on the manure heap and turning its head slowly and wisely back and forth, and it seemed to me that I had been standing for eternity and looking at the bird. I had lost consciousness of time and space and was appalled by the smallest gesture of human life — — even that behind me."

The last words, separated by a pause, were spoken by Weitfeld with a grave tone.

"So. By that do you mean the conversation between Mrs Forstmeister and myself?" his wife asked, taken aback.

"Yes," was Weitfeld's decisive answer.

"But we were speaking of the war."

"Yes, yes. I know. Just for that reason."

"No, that can't be! Husband, listen! Millions are dying and millions are being crippled. And you say that is nothing more than whether a crow is turning its head back and forth. Man!"

Mrs Weitfeld sprang towards her husband, seized him with both hands and shook him. Her full bust swelled and her voice trembled. "That is nonsense! That is nonsense!", she repeated until tears came into her eyes. Then she let go of him, sat down on a chair by the window and cried soundlessly into her hands. Professor Weitfeld had turned pale. But he just clasped his hands behind his back again, taking no step towards his wife, but just looking with knitted brow at the gentle movement of her shoulders. Then he said softly, "Yes, you are right. It is nonsense, that is, to seek some sense behind this war."

Then he waited for an answer.

But his wife did not take her hands from her face.

For that reason, the Professor stepped softly to his writing desk, sat down in his chair, propped his arms on its back and looked musingly before himself into the room which had become so still that you could hear the flies knocking against the window pane with a soft pecking sound.

"What sense has it that Russia has risen up and what sense that it has disintegrated? Do you know? Does a man, any man in the world truly know? I don't know."

Weitfeld was speaking as if he were alone and talking to himself.

"Thousands upon thousands of freedom fanatics are pining there in the hells of Siberia and being strangled at the gallows and now they who have suffered under the Tsar's oppression are rampaging with the same means against their fellow men, entirely the same as those which once drove them to outrage. Is their perhaps sense in that?"

His wife tore her face out from her hands and said hostilely, "What concern are the Russians to me?"

"Hm. — Yes. —" the Professor replied after some thought. "You're right. But, if we Germans deem the Russians as not worthy of human consideration, how can we be filled with indignation that the French, English and Americans no longer count *us* among humans?"

The blond woman by the window did not know how to reply to that, propped her hands on her knees with stiff arms and looked darkly before herself with her pale, shaken face on whose cheeks tears still stood.

"We did not want this war, did not start it," she said after a while dully.

"Oh woman, let's leave out this talk from the newspapers. Christ is not to blame for Christianity as it is today, and nevertheless it originates from him. Why does a spring break out of the ground in a specific place? How does a storm arise? How does a leaf grow? We invent the reasons for it afterwards. It never tallies. And how it stands with the affairs of nature, so it behaves with the affairs of men. And what was the sense of the Ptolemaic realm? Why did the state of Montezuma arise and die away? Why did Peru prosper? All these great events are today not as important as the pecking sound of summer flies on the window of this quiet room.

Dear woman, and the day after tomorrow in a hundred thousand years, this war in which we now live will also have been so and idle men will tell tales of the sense, the presumed sense of this catastrophe, without getting to the bottom of it, just as we struggle in vain."

"And what do you want to say about that?" his wife asked.

"You will hear it forthwith. When a hundred thousand men scream 'ah', it remains 'ah'. If a single person emitted this sound, then it is not transformed thereby. We believe, however, that when a hundred thousand scream 'ah', every single one is transformed. And when a man murders another, we call it a crime. The murder of millions, however, should be an act over which we should be pleased. You expect in the future from it brilliance and greatness.

My dear Manja, isn't such thought nonsense and if the *thought* is, does not also the *action* have to be?"

His wife had risen noiselessly, clutched the back of the chair tightly with her right hand and was looking at her husband with an expression of horror. The Professor looked up at her for a long time with an anguished face and then moved his gaunt head with an amicably bitter smile around his lips, as if he were nodding drowsily.

"Do you see, dear, — and I? I will not spring at you now, as you did before, rattle you by the shoulders and shout, 'Isn't that nonsense?' — But I beg, sit down, I want to tell you why I came, through the sight of a crow, to all this which I have now said to you. When I saw as it were the greyish black bird in the flickering light outside, sitting in the field, an experience that I had on my last Sinai trip crossed my mind.

We came out of the Wadi Faran and turned into the Wadi Mokatteb. The valley of the inscriptions. The further we penetrated into this flat, sandy depression, the more the inscriptions accumulated on the stones of the hillside, which never rose to great heights. For the large part, we saw Nabataean lettering, in between there were also figurative depictions of the most primitive sort, like those children or quite primitive ethnic groups tend to produce. But the dry air had preserved everything wonderfully in the soft stone, although more than two thousand years had passed since their origin.

Riding along the Wadi, my old Abu ben Mahmud brought my attention to fresh tracks in the sand. I climbed down curiously and investigated the indentations of European footwear. Then I said to myself that it was all the same anyway who had been here a short time ago next to his camel, straightened up and let my eyes glide contemplatively along the walls dotted with inscriptions until where the Wadi was narrowed by a bump in the ground and almost blocked off.

When I lifted my eyes thus from the glimmering embers slowly over the rocks into the immaculate blue of the endless, deep sky, a mounted Bedouin was standing, as if he had grown out of the earth, on the ridge of the hill. His grey-white horse was blowing its breath through its nostrils and raising a leg to swoop down. The rider was leaning forward attentively. His head wound with a white cloth, his long rifle lying across his lap, he looked at us for a while. And as I saw him standing thus against the sky in his wild audacity and steely resolve, the thought seared through me that he was a soldier of that long lapsed kingdom from whose time the lettering on the stones had been left behind. The air seemed to tremble from the faint noise of distant martial weaponry. The signs inscribed on the stones suddenly looked strangely fresh, as if they had been inscribed days ago and not thousands of years ago, and I would not have been amazed if the rider had leapt down and, pointing at a stone, said to me, 'Do you see the man with the snout here sitting on the throne? It was none other than the accursed rebel whose sword scratched this picture in the stone to mock our illustrious lord and his warriors. The Wadi is still full of the pestilent breath of his horde who came through it. My animal itself is disgusted by being in the air which these rejects have corrupted, for it blows the breath from itself like a poison that it has sucked up and shakes so that it almost throws me from its back. But just wait, you outcasts, before the night has cooled this desert three times, your heads will be lying about silently like the stones of this Wadi here.'

I was still surrounded by this imaginary conceit when the man whom I had dreamt as a soldier was already next to me and old Mahmud. He was a man of the Djebeline tribe and hunting for a panther which had been troubling a not so distant oasis for days. He soon got into a conversation with Mahmud and promised he would sell us a goat for our evening meal in his village, which we intended reaching before nightfall.

You see, Manja, all times seem thus like a breath before the eternity within us, before our souls. And should we be so foolish as to exaggerate the breath which just now skims past us, even if it is with the thunder of a thousand iron barrels?"

His wife sat there with her hands folded in her lap and her head lowered pensively. She was breathing heavily but, speaking no word, rose noiselessly after a while and took a few steps towards him as if she wanted to give her husband a calm, collected answer. Suddenly she threw her hands up, pressed them against her temples and screamed despairingly and tormentedly, "Never! No! No! No, no!" Then she plunged out the door, ran down the hall as though chased and stormed up the stairs.

Weitfeld watched her with every sign of disappointment, then rose slowly, closed the door, bolted it from within and began strolling back and forth in the room.

2

To begin with, his gait was restless, his steps uneven. He often stroked his lightly greying, formerly blond, pointed beard with his left hand and drew it all the way to the last hair through the shaking fingers of his thin, limpid hand.

Gradually his step lengthened and eased, and his lean body bent a little each time his foot left the floor.

After he had thus been stepping back and forth in his room for a good hour, he pulled up slowly like a clock petering out. The swings of the pendulum become smaller, wearier and finally the balance spring exhales the last barely perceivable creak. Weitfeld covered his high, wrinkled forehead with his hand, as if to calm it through a cool wrapper, and shut his eyes at the same time, as if it passed for stilling the mining of a secret anguish, and murmured after a long deliberation, "It's right to wrestle oneself away from the mutilation through the external. For the problem of life involves displacing the activity deeper and deeper into ourselves. That is the only way to freedom, the only possibility for this eternal, fundamental requirement of mankind to finally become fact."

Then he let his hands fall and looked in a sort of bewildered astonishment into nothingness, whereby he pursed his lips to whistle and made such large, dazed eyes that his brows were almost shoved halfway up his forehead.

"Yeees," he said, letting out his held breath, "someone on this confused earth must make a start with it. And why in all the world should I not be that one?"

After that he looked along the wall of his room, which was filled up with bookshelves right up almost to the ceiling, obtaining thereby a mocking smile in his face, walked slowly to it and drew the greyish green curtain across the colourful, gold printed volumes. The brass rings slid whirring over the iron rod and he softly repeated the admonition constantly, "But for God's sake, not to think again. Not — to — think — a — gain."

Thus he went murmuring from one bookcase to another. In the end, he also drew the light curtains together across the balcony door and all the windows, sat down at his writing table in the yellowish green dimness and delved into the viewing of a page on which he had drawn a circle on whose inner perimeter a pentagon had been placed, and inside that again a triangle. The first figure was inked out in blue, the second in brown, the triangle in green. It was the sort he had attuned for months to the new melody, to the universal human powers. He sat leaning back in his chair, his forearms lying on his thighs with flat, outstretched hands. He looked thus fixedly with falling face at the drawing. From time to time, he shut his eyes for a long time to "suck in to perfect predominance in the depths" of his vision of the figures.

After perhaps an hour, he heard a tentative knocking on the door and the maidservant calling, which he had not answered, and then the knocking had been repeated, "Professor, the Lady wishes to say, it is served."

Weitfeld did not stir.

A while later, children's steps pattered on the wooden stairs, came on tiptoe to the door, stopped at the threshold and after a breath through the keyhole and suppressed giggle, the door was abruptly knocked on again and a boy's voice said timidly, "Father, the soup is getting cold."

Weitfeld knitted his eyebrows reluctantly, rose and said, "Girl and boy!"

"Yes," came the double-voiced reply.

"Tell mother I am meditating and don't want to be disturbed until I inform otherwise. Do you understand, Jörg?"

"Yes, father."

"Good. So until later."

The children whirled freely along the hall, up the stairs, and he soon heard them in the dining room above him moving the chairs.

But he went and stretched himself out on the chaise longue and shut his eyes.

A dreamily soft swishing was in his head, like he had often experienced in the tropics during his Oriental journeys when, sleepless in the night in the desert, he had heard the fine sand driving against the walls of his tent.

After a long time, the chairs were again moving above him. Then it was still and Weitfeld knew that his children were now saying the composition which he had taught them with much effort. And as if he were sitting with them and having to help them over the difficult parts, he spoke half out loud and with pedantically exact accentuation the words of his verse to himself in the green darkness,

> Newly inflamed by the meal,
> It leads us to new transformation.
> Our life becomes ever constantly
> More rounded through action.
>
> The created is created
> Again in our spirits,
> Until the active amassing
> Leads to the circling of all.
>
> Human striving must never
> Recover in its own bounds,
> For our life forces us restlessly
> To ever higher brilliance.

So swing me newly inflamed
Ever further, comrades,
Until the being binds itself lightly
Free in today's yet to be.

Up above, it then continued now and then, sometimes with heavy steps that rattled the ceiling lamp softly, probably the maidservant; sometimes with soft skips, presumably the children. He listened to the steps and thought at the same time about the content of the verse. When it had become quite still, he got half up and said almost loudly like a strict command the last two lines into the dead silence of his room,

Until the being binds itself lightly
Free in today's yet to be.

He mused for a long time at the floor, nodded to himself in severe resolution, lay back down and, after a few moments, fell asleep.

3

When Weitfeld awoke, he noticed in the reddened light which was falling through the hazy green of the curtains that it had already passed into evening. He sat up and, as if he were rising from his night's sleep and required, in order to find his way into the day, knowledge of the dreams which had led him through his sleep, he referred back with his mind. But he saw nothing but the conflict with his wife, considered her behaviour and his words, and noted that the arguments which he had brought up were quite poor in regard to his great, newly won conviction and had fallen out somewhat confusedly, and that, measured against the height of his idea, his new lifestyle could seem odd perhaps to outsiders, yes, who knows, perhaps even must seem so.

Only it could not have been otherwise. The floor on which he moved was new, hence it was no wonder he behaved, even to himself, at the moment somewhat strangely. For to enact a new age for humanity, it was not really absolutely necessary and appropriate to skip the midday meal and then sleep through the entire afternoon. The exultation of his wife, especially her screaming and running around, the laughter of his children behind the door, everything was quite natural. He rose smiling and said to himself that the problem of perfect appropriateness or better congruence between the inner world and the outer life circumstances could never be achieved by a man. From this incongruence, absolutely all conceivability, all visibility, all perceptibility originated, and that formed the basis for the fact that everyone, even such a venerable man, is on exact perusal a comical figure.

Laughing, he stretched his arms above himself and said loudly, "But for that reason, we do not take our hand from the plough!"

Then he opened the curtains to all the windows, even to the balcony door, so that the full light of the slanting sun streamed into the room, listened to the quiet house, and then stepped to the writing desk to meditate for a moment yet on his orientation page, the drawing of the three geometric figures. Satisfied, he put it away.

Oh no, success was undeniable. Weeks ago he had taken himself in hand again and was no longer the playground of eternal unrest, horror, grim anguish, and a burdensome sorrow.

He had simply stepped out of the bloody circle.

"So it must be," he murmured, closing the drawer of his desk and leaving the house by the

back door. On stepping down the few steps lead-
ing into the garden, a light spell of dizziness
befogged him. A florid swimming came over his
brain and the bushes leaning over the narrow
gravel path lost their distinct outlines and looked
like a green wave of water flowing down soundlessly onto the yellow sand. The Professor laid
his cool hand on his forehead, took hold of the
path with firm steps and walked, already perfectly free and steady again, through the little
gate onto the village path which ran along the
bank of the Zacken. He had the feeling his wife
was watching him from the window of her room.
But he did not turn around, instead recalling that
Manja was visiting Mrs Forstmeister that afternoon. So this mysterious feeling of being
scanned on his back had probably deceived him,
and it was just "a misguided, rambling thought of
unease manifesting itself there in the illusion of a
sensed stimulus." With a gaze felt strangely from
within, half turned to stride onward, he looked at
the high, red tile roof of the Forstmeisters' which
could be seen next to his villa between the wide
branched treetops of old broad-leafed trees and,
as stark as lightning, the memory of a scene from
half a year before was before his mind. It had
been a hard morning with mercilessly clear,
frosty, wintery sun. Trees and bushes formed a
single white wave. The steps of pedestrians
crunched, a high whimpering came up from under the runners of sleds and pulled along puffing

behind the passengers. Standing by the window of his well-heated bedroom, he had looked out into this newly coated in snow, bitterly cold December day and noticed after a while old Käse, the enthusiast for all the world's handicrafts, from Johnsbach, who provided the office of porter to the houses of the propertied and with the locality's summer vacation guests. With a little sled which he was dragging carefully behind him, he turned from the back gate of the Forst-meisters' garden onto the path, closed the little gate so that the latch rattled loudly, stepped onto the little sled and fiddled with the cords which fastened a broad, flat, wooden chest to it. Then he trotted with his laborious, slow trot down-stream along the Zacken path, throwing a look, on reaching Weitfeld's garden gate, at the Pro-fessor's house as if he had a request, but barely paused for a slowed step and then went busily onward. By some mysterious turn in his inner being, this behaviour of the old man had seemed strange to the Professor at the time and, as if sit-ting in ambush, he had then more than ever taken up post to observe what would happen next. After the passing of barely ten minutes, his wife had stepped in impassioned excitement out the same back garden gate of the Forstmeisters' property through which the old porter Käse had just come; she had looked down the Zacken path as if she were looking after the spry old man and then, falling into a wild, whirling run, she had fled back through the garden into the house as if she were a mad teenager and not the ten-years-married wife of the university professor Josef Weitfeld. At the place on the white snow covered Zacken path directly opposite the little gate, however, where Käse had paused, and to which his wife had looked for a moment after the departing man, a crow had settled down a little while afterwards with clammy, ill-tempered flight, blown its feathers up into a greyish black ball and eyed with head askew sometimes the one, sometimes the other side for sustenance.

The memory of this incident took possession of the Professor unawares like lightning and was loaded with such a threatening momentousness that he continued walking, shaking his head and asking himself in vain what sort of meaning it had.

When he had reached the first bridge over the Zacken, he paused, brooding, and he was beset by the suspicion that this incident was possibly the mysterious basis for why, this morning during the conversation between his wife and Mrs Forstmeister, the crow had appeared so strange on the manure heap far out in the field. "We will shortly be able to see what lay behind it," he said to himself and threw a glance over the bridge, on which just then a girl of about ten had emerged from the other side and was approaching him.

The child, probably coming from a poor family, hung thin and frail like a little, living corpse in her patched up, short little dress, and when she was standing by him and had heard his question about whether old Käse lived around there, she gave him the desired information with such a soft, frosty voice, while pointing with outstretched hand over the river to the confusion of little houses, that the Professor felt his heart clench bitterly because he noted how this innocent child had been emaciated as a consequence of the war. For that reason, Weitfeld's well-developed, tall body did not set itself in motion, as was its custom, with a distracted nod of the head, without thanks or greeting in the direction given, instead he pulled down the outstretched arm of the child, pressed two ten pfennig coins into the hand, and said with expressive voice at the same time the first two lines of his verse composition:

> Newly inflamed by the meal,
> It leads us to new transformation.

He then nodded to her meaningfully once more and then strode across the bridge without paying attention to the bewilderment of the girl who now looked towards the tall, gaunt man with the lightly dipping upper body, then at the two blackish coins, took on a look of light merriment in her face and then sprang down the path by the little river, laughing and singing.

Weitfeld walked through the clutter of Hühnersteige Way, between the little houses into the enclosed garden, went around where there was nothing to go around, looked around attentively where there was nothing remarkable to be seen, smiled winningly at strange faces, gauged indifferent men with threatening eyes, and had constantly the feeling close to his sore heart again that he had to draw his hand out of a crunching gearbox which was racing around him and snapping at him with a thousand iron gear wheels.

Finally he stood before Käse's house, which crouched like a large tortoise, broad and grey in the greenery like the other premises too, covered with aged shingles, and only one row of windows, barely a child's height above the ground. When he stepped across the little forecourt, which was no bigger than an outspread travel rug, he thought, 'Even if I don't want to, I will remain safe despite all mischief.' With this flittering in his head, he stepped into the single large room of the house, which, very spacious, very modest and painstakingly clean, lay completely in the green dimness of the foliage obscured windows. Old Käse, probably just returned from a walk, was sitting at the scrubbed white, enormous table, brushing the sweat from his brow with the one hand and searching in his trouser pocket with the other for his money purse to count out his day's proceeds. He had placed his green flat cap with the brass badge of office on the table. When the entering Professor appeared in the open doorway, he drew back his hand, which wanted to travel into his pocket, reached for his cap, his official attire, moved his already quite shrunken body as if he wanted to rise, and even before Weitfeld had greeted him, said with a helpful smile, "A beautiful good evening too and what would be needed, sir, if I may ask?" But now he recognised the man entering for the first time and added quickly, "Ah, is that you, Professor?"

"Yes," Weitfeld answered, "quite right. It is me," and stepped to the table, carefully eyeing little Käse who was crouched on a chair like a little heap of humanity.

"You are the porter, Käse, aren't you? Yes. I see. Quite right. If I now come to you, it is not actually necessary that I come to you because it is succinctly put in a poem, 'The striving of man must never capture itself in its own bounds.' Only last Winter before Christmas, you put a package in the post to Berlin for my wife. From the Forstmeisters'. Is that right?"

The old porter was bewildered. "Hmm. How do you mean? Quite right. A package. No, no. That's right. Before Christmas. Well indeed. That's right, mother, before Christmas it was, when I took the picture ... This is my wife."

Mrs Käse, also small, old, but still plump and animated, had appeared in the doorway during the stammering of her husband and was now walking past the Professor to the table. A long exchange began immediately between the old couple about unimportant trivialities, only because both were frightened that the entire affair was hiding in its folds a danger or at least a disadvantage for them.

Weitfeld listened for a while silently. Then he grasped in his pocket, laid a fifty on the table and said decidedly, "Alright. Thank you. My wife had no change at the time. Fifty pfennig was the remainder. Here it is."

With a glance at the money, the face of the old porter brightened.

"No, no, if that is so, then, as they say, Professor, everything tallies. Of course, of course." With these words, he took the money calmly into his hand.

Weitfeld shut his eyes and turned his suddenly pale, suffering face to the ceiling. Then he murmured, "The crow."

"What did you say?" Mrs Käse asked, observing his strange behaviour with astonishment.

But Weitfeld had himself in hand again already. "The matter is thus settled," he said dolefully. "You have received the fifty pfennigs for the picture. Good evening."

He turned around, stooped his tall body under the low doorway and vanished with his dipping gait into the bushes of Hühnersteige Way towards the Zacken bridge.

Old Käse had risen and was watching his departure from the window.

"Being educated is not good and over-educated no good at all," he said and scratched the back of his head at the same time. "That is a horse with five legs, mother, the Professor from Berlin," he continued his meditation, turning around.

"What did it have to do with you then, eh?" his better half asked dismissively.

"No, no, mother, I'm not racking my brain over it either. But, you understand, it tallied to the penny with his wife and now the gentleman comes, gives me a fifty and makes off again and for all that, he talks and makes eyes as if he had a chimney in his body."

"Oh, Käse, that has nothing to do with you," his wife replied. "It is the war. It carries on up and down out there, in every village and in every head. You're a porter and when anyone gives you more then you take it and keep your mouth shut."

"Well no. Certainly not. I won't. Ha! What's going on with the Professor and his wife has nothing to do with me. No, no. You're right, mother. Certainly not."

Thus again grumbling more to himself than speaking to his wife, who was not listening to him anymore either, the old man had dawdled across the room. On the threshold, he turned around once more and said, "No, no, mother. If the plaster falls from the church, it has nothing to do with the bell ringer. I alone know." Laughing out loud, he stepped out of the house, leant over the fence and looked for the Professor, whom he saw just then walking over the Zacken bridge, his head bowed as if the low timber ceiling was still over it.

4

The evening had meanwhile advanced further. The Sudeten Mountains, that melodious, high, beautifully curved procession of mountains, lay in a calm light that was full of a mild haze, and at the same time, a morbid garishness, a garishness which, like the approaching fever of an open wound, you do not perceive with the eyes, but experience with the inner sight. Strewn here and there over the clear sky, opalescent, round clouds stood in perfect motionlessness, with a soft blush breathed over them like startled, helpless faces rising from a bad dream. The mountains, however, alternated their colours as though from an inner urge, sometimes breathing a smoky grey, sometimes sunken in a deep blue, sometimes overrun with a dull red so that they lost all firmness, disappearing, emerging and then seeming to stream away inexorably again.

Weitfeld paused a few times on his way, turned around and sank into the experience of this soundless, cosmic unrest in the heights, shook his head and then walked onward, again persistently looking just in front of his feet. "Strange," he murmured, "most strange." And then he thought of a verse from his composition:

The created is created
Again in our spirits.

With that he made a move, which was just as restless and phantasmal as in the depths of the sky before him, from the middle of the path to the Zacken, leant across the handrail and stared with the dissolute eyes of an inwardly disintegrating man at the water drawing past in softly gleaming waves.

A field grey soldier, whose one leg was shortened and the other stiff, was shuffling past laboriously on two walking sticks. Because he saw the distinguished gentleman looking down so tensely at the water, he also hobbled over to find out what was so remarkable there. When he had been looking down for a while, he received such a twinge in his twice-shot leg that he groaned softly. Then Weitfeld turned around, saw his painfully contorted countenance, and blanched, but got a hold of himself and asked kindheartedly and gently, "Tell me please, do you also hear the peculiar, dull rumbling of the waves? Water must be pouring from underground into the Zacken here. For there are currents under the surface that are often stronger than the upper ones into which they flow, currents which drive our mills and all such odds and ends."

The last words, he had spoken entirely to himself again, entirely in the darkness of his inner disturbance.

The soldier surveyed him with a critical look, shrugged his shoulders, spat into the water and said indifferently, "Oh well."

Weitfeld stared tensely at the waves, turned around after a long while, and asked, "What? — And to see is nothing anyway, just nothing. Even if you pay attention carefully. No man really notices anything suspicious. Strange, most strange, strange."

Without pay any further attention to the soldier, he walked onward, head lowered, dipping up and down.

"Hey, comrade, hey!" the field grey man now called after him.

The Professor stopped and looked back with a perfectly absent look.

"Is it right, you've been buried?" the soldier asked and endeavoured to hobble over hurriedly.

Weitfeld, who did not understand the field grey man's words in his self-absorption, shook his head, waved him away with his hand, and walked onward, immediately lapsing into sobbing.

"Manja, my wife ... everything is obviously of no use to me ... yes ... my wife ... haha ... I know

... of course ... so and yet not ..." he murmured mutely to himself.

Then he stepped into a short street which gently climbed upward.

After a few minutes, he was standing before the villa of the retired Consul Griepenstein. When he entered the little garden, he saw the seventy six year old man sitting, lounging back on a chair and looking up full of blissful abandonment into the treetop of a maple on whose uppermost tips a blackbird was singing into the glow of the red evening. His face was framed by a short-kept, completely white beard and bore widely progressed features of senile childishness. With the tip of his right foot, he was tapping the rhythm of the birdsong and with the fingers of both hands, he was drumming a military march on the steel top of the little garden table which stood before him.

Weitfeld had entered cautiously through the little gate, threw a glance at the rapt old man, who just then laughed out loud, and then roamed about everywhere with his eyes.

When he did not discern Griepenstein's daughter, he wanted to withdraw again. But with the turning of his feet, the sand crunched. The consul started, saw the somewhat disconcerted Professor and came storming towards him with outspread arms.

"Ah. Hoho, what a surprise? Most obedient, most obedient servant of all, dear, dear Professor!" he sputtered effusively. "Charming, charming! Just listen though to the dear little birds. They know it. They have sensed it. God, I have been sitting for half an hour already, letting the heavens make music over me and thinking of my dear fatherland. In the red gold of evening ... in the red gold of evening ... in the red ... yes ..."

Weitfeld made not a sound, was led by the lively old man to the little table and pressed into a chair.

It was different now from what he had expected. The old man paid not the slightest attention to the Professor's state, but began immediately an endless, outwardly excited argument with himself over the hardships and fortunes of Germany, especially the present fortune and the attack into the sun which had hopefully dismissed every half and complete coward for ever, "apparently torn apart in the middle, never to be patched up again." Then the old soldier got stuck grimly into Prince Lichnowsky, who had by the publication of his London legation activities caused such serious embarrassment for the central powers, called him a diplomatic infant, sprang from Count Beer into the midst of the strategy of Clausewitz, Moltke and Schlieffen and prattled around for a while there between antiquated quotations and doctrines. Now and then, he interrupted himself, touched Weitfeld's arm, smiled at him from below with mischievous childishness and asked, "No? Am I not right? Or are you of a different opinion, say it quietly. Whoever becomes old like me can not be blown over so easily, hahaha! No. So, as I just said ..." and then it continued in the old way again.

The Professor sat quite still, looked through the leaves of the tree at the sky burning deeper and deeper, soon felt sleepy, and thought, 'But f Malva would just come so that a decision could be made — damned Griepenstein, the idiot, is pure acid.'

"Am I not right, Professor?" the consul asked again just then.

"Yes," Weitfeld finally answered to the bewilderment of the old man, looked at him kindly, and thought, 'Now I've had enough.' He continued out loud, "Perfectly of your opinion, Consul. It is, as you have just now correctly proven, absolutely the same when a madman strikes as when he is struck by another madman."

"Allow me most kindly, dear sir. You must have misheard. I was speaking just then of the advantages of the skewed front," Griepenstein interjected.

"Just so. And I was just applying the fact of the skewedness to another sphere."

The Consul's mouth stood open and smiling helplessly he said, "Ah so. Hmhm. Please tell me again, dear sir."

But Weitfeld was already sitting quietly with a motionless, sorrowful face as if he had not taken an interest in Griepenstein's own words. After a few moments, however, he sensed that the old man had spoken to him and said, "Rightly so, Consul. You will also know about the perpetual phenomenon of the strange acoustics of consciousness towards all the sounds of fate. Nevertheless it is known to all thinking men that all spiritual apperception is only a perfect, never a present tense, thus it surprises men ever anew, and indeed not always pleasantly, to first perceive fate when it has already happened. And when we settle down for a barrage, my dear soldier, we battle not with a present evil, but with the consequences of one already past."

As he said this, the Professor had stood up, for he had heard steps coming into the garden.

"Yes, yes. That is the thing, dear Consul," he said softly, and tapped him laughing on the shoulder. Griepenstein remained huddled up and asked stuttering, "Then you mean we don't know why we are fighting. Or what? I don't understand you."

At this moment, Miss Griepenstein stepped out of the bushes. Weitfeld ignored the Consul's grave questions. "Ah, here is Miss Malva!" he exclaimed. "Hello, Miss Griepenstein. You are looking quite aglow. You have surely come from your painting. I know about it from Manja. Her face then is always as if it were facing into the red of evening," and he walked quickly up to her.

"Good evening, Professor," the old maid said somewhat slowly. "Very nice that you're visiting us. Yes. Is your Manja painting again too?"

At this moment, the old Consul, who had been sitting there brooding, flared up with great indignation, drew his daughter to the side and whispered in her ear, "Dear, the Professor is crazy." Then he turned to Weitfeld, made a deep bow with a smile, waved humbly with his hand and said most ingratiatingly, "Your most loyal servant, dear Professor!" At that he vanished into the bushes from where soon afterwards a loud laughter echoed.

"Yes, my father is downright wild today because of that unprecedentedly magnificent Western offensive," Malva Griepenstein said, gazing after him. "He has become really young."

"You are right there, Miss, truly youthful."

"No? And then he is ever thankful if he can express himself to someone. For he has been alone a long time, you sense that Egon's death made him not quite right."

The painter, whilst speaking in her mealy way, was steering her slow steps towards the entrance to the garden because she was of the opinion that Weitfeld wanted to go home again.

The Professor followed her, always remaining half a step behind, looked with pale face at the ground, and with each step, he stabbed a few holes with his cane in the sand around the sole of his boot.

"Where did your brother fall?" he asked half aloud without raising his head.

"At Baranovichi as a battery commander," the painter answered. "Yes. A dazzling future ... and now? If it had just not thrown mother so, it could still continue."

She was standing before the gate. The Professor now raised his gaze and fixed it on Malva Griepenstein so sharply that, as was her habit, she closed her large, ever salivating mouth and blinked teasingly with her somewhat reddened, lashless eyes.

"What did you want to say, Professor?" she asked sweetly, because he was still staring at her face.

"I did not come here especially for that reason," Weitfeld finally said softly and paled even more with a slight twitching of his face.

"No? I thought the house would have become too narrow even with patriotic joy, and with the joy of your father, you would have ..."

Weitfeld interrupted her almost roughly.

"No," he said, "I came because of you and now you are here, you are throwing me in this noiseless way immediately back into the street," and laughed.

"Oh no, you jest, dear sir," the old Miss replied blushing, "and at the same time, you speak that mischief with such a deathly serious face. So please, tell me ..."

Whilst Malva said that somewhat hastily, she shut the gate and went back into the garden.

Weitfeld followed her.

"Absolutely no malice, dear Miss," he said behind her. "No, if the residents of Berlin admire your pictures, it is no mischief if I as a resident of Johnsbach want to see them too."

Now Malva blossomed. Her languorous manner vanished. She walked sinuously to the house entrance, "Ah, I didn't know at all how nice you can be, and then Manja always says you don't care at all for the art of painting. Allow me to walk ahead of you. We must be quick. It is good light just now. Please, here, Mr Weitfeld!"

Malva led the way eagerly. She spoke the last words a little muffled and then slipped on her toes into the large painting room, scurried through to the door to the next room and shut it carefully.

"So," she then said exhaling, "mother is sitting next door in the recliner and towards evening she always sleeps for an hour."

Weitfeld laid his hat and stick on the table and took a seat on a chair with understanding nods while Malva Griepenstein moved the easel with the large picture out of the evening glow. It was a park landscape by moonlight, with the shadowy mass of a castle in the background, from whose windows little clumps of red light were appended, on the whole an obtrusive, fat pig of a painting.

"Speaking candidly, Manja treasures you a lot, Miss Malva, as you know yourself," Weitfeld said, and he now stepped closer to the picture, then fixed his eyes, seemingly acutely, on it from a distance. At the same time, he spoke muffled, measured, and obligingly. "Yes, really excellent, the blurring of the tree tops whipped by the wind. Yes, what I wanted to say, Manja treasures you a lot. Only she thinks that if you would give up your broad manner of painting in favour of a precise, concentrated stroke then your success would be yet magnified."

He dropped his pince nez and looked sharply over to her. What he had expected occurred. She blanched and broke out softly into a mocking laughter.

For since she had had success, the otherwise so self-composed, almost indolent old maid had become extremely vulnerable. She held her pictures to be works of art and claimed to only sell to serious connoisseurs, although through the mediation of bustling men, her sole takers were the new rich of the capital, the war profiteers. She wrinkled her nose over exhibitions and continued painting grandiose, colourful, novelistic landscapes.

"Yes, Manja, your dear wife. Hahaha!" she laughed bitingly. "Then she should just put her pictures before real connoisseurs and she will see who is right."

"I came here just because of that, dear Miss, to form a judgment from my own inspection. I find your stroke fresh, almost furiously passionate. So that you would think another being has painted this picture, not you, this dear, gentle Malva."

"No? And how do you like the ghosting moonlight?" she asked, flattered.

"Very much and how richly nuanced! No. there Manja is wrong. But she is not to be won over to your style. In addition she only ever gives her pictures to friends who then only impair her by being nice and polite."

Miss Griepenstein looked at the Professor's gaunt face with surprise as it became more and more suffering.

"I mean it just as I say it," he said in answer to her incredulous hesitation. Then he took his seat again at the table and continued, "You must know that I am in favour of serious, physical work, even if Manja views painting now as the chief task of her life."

Malva laughed maliciously.

"May I openly tell you my opinion?" she asked then and sat down quite close to him.

"I will even ask for it," the Professor answered, sensed that the sweat was rising on his forehead and lightly brushed across his face with his handkerchief.

"You are perfectly right," Malva said and laid her hand on his arm. "This dependence on acquaintances and friends, with their hallelujahs for everything that comes from Manja, impairs her directly. Above all that assessor, Körten. The man really somersaulted when I gave him Manja's little picture at Easter in the Görlitz train station. Quite senseless with delight, he was. Even without having seen it, he named Manja with Liebermann and Klinger and Thoma and who knows who, in one breath."

While Malva was saying that with great excitement, she saw the Professor automatically smiling, despite this merriment though, his face was becoming more and more sorrowfull. Then he rose soundlessly and stiffly.

Miss Griepenstein saw that he was intending to go into the living room but was suddenly paralysed.

Then he laughed with such merriment that Malva recalled the suspicion of her father who had considered the Professor crazy, and she cried, "God, what is it with you then? You are staggering, Professor!"

In fear her voice climbed almost to a scream.

Weitfeld stretched his arm out and took a couple of staggering steps towards the hearth, continually laughing bravely.

From the adjoining room, short sobbing sounds rang out, like the hollow yapping of an abandoned hunting dog, "hu — hu — hu — hu — hu."

"What is that?" Weitfeld inquired, reaching the hearth which he now leant on.

"Oh you know, now that is the terrible thing. She is paralysed and since Egon's death no longer of sound mind. As soon as she awakes, she cries so impotently and raggedly day and night over Egon. But what was happening with you just then?"

"It is nothing much," he answered, cheering up. "I can't tolerate the war food and even sometimes become faint with hunger. But everything is okay again now. A pity that we are so hampered in this conversation. No, you are perfectly correct in your views over my wife. Thank you and I will seek to have an affect on Manja."

While he was speaking, the poor madwoman yapped continuously in the adjoining room, monotonously sobbing, "hu — hu — hu — hu —".

The Professor took up his hat and stick with studious care, listened to the crying of the old woman, and left out with sorrowful despondency on his face.

5

On the way home, the Professor fell into thought in the fields towards Wernersdorf, fled before a troop of war-blind who, led by a sister, were singing a school song and walking towards the Hermsdorf train station, and arrived home late at night, almost driven to exhaustion. Everyone was already asleep. Without lighting a candle, he toddled up the steps to the upper floor, looked in the dining room for something edible and devoured greedily everything that had been left for him on the table. He did all that in complete darkness, because he was frightened of starkly recognising in the brightness of the storm of his impassioned thoughts and in his condition that which he must avoid because it contradicted his newfound life principle of being led by the relativity of sharp, purely intellectual knowledge. He wanted everything decided by his last, divine instance, by his soul, not to act arbitrarily, but to affect only the uninfluenced impulse of his fate. As he walked through the hallway to his bedroom, which lay next to his study, he felt his body become like a dim sheaf of light in the darkness and inferred from this incomprehensible phenomenon that with this new capability for action, puzzling to himself, he was on the right path.

Whilst undressing he pondered that the most men's confusion in their state of being was because of the irritability with themselves that no one on earth could spring over their own shadow, but most of them stumbled over it and fell down. The shadows of our being, however, are our thoughts about ourselves. To eschew them means to go out of the way of the destruction of life and to bring the other side of all short circuits of causality to a unity.

With this new "composition", he climbed into bed, drew the covers over himself and, before he had twice turned over, sank down into a strange dream which lasted the entire night.

At the end, he awoke with a scream.

It was already late in the morning.

The sun was filling the entire room, and his clothes lay strewn over the floor as if he had undressed whilst walking around the previous evening and had let every single piece of clothing fall carelessly to the floor where he stood.

"Was I dreaming?" the Professor asked himself and, shaking his head in disbelief, looked over the mess of clothes spread across the floor.

"... perhaps already before I climbed into bed, while I was still walking around the table," he continued his disbelief.

No, that could not be, for he still recalled sharply the new composition of his new view of life. Or if that was not the case, then his clothes were actually lying as always, neatly arranged on the chair at the foot of his bed, and what he saw there on the floor was just his imagination. He grasped at the chair and found that it was empty.

"Yes, my God!" he said excitedly and attempted to climb out of bed to convince himself whether they really were clothes which lay there on the floor. But strange. He was unable to move his arms or legs. It was as if they had been hacked off or had gone away.

"Did I dream that?" he asked, doubting his perception again. But all at once, the entire dream stood starkly before his eyes in all its details, loomed up and, in the next seconds, had vanished again.

The consequences of this affair consisted in that he was now lying in bed as if really maimed; stiff and shaken. "No," he said softly, "that was no dream, that was of course a truth which is so hidden that it could not reveal itself except in mysterious sleeping images to my spirit. — And if it revealed something, then during my sleep, someone else must have *seen* into me. And isn't seeing alert living? Good. So sleep means just another way of being awake and living." And when he had gotten this far with his far removed drilling, he again felt inwardly dismembered into two worlds like in the last part of his dream, in which he had been frightened into the awakening by his external sight. And the clothes on the floor appeared to him like a senseless remnant of his being which he did not trust himself to crawl back into.

He wrapped the covers tightly around himself, lay down on his back and looked with large, lost eyes for a long time at the ceiling.

"Hm," he murmured after a long while. "*Toxicatmicus*. Well yes. Perhaps. *Toxicocolica*. — Is quite possible. *Toxicolog*. It'll be that. Yes, yes."

And he drew his right hand from under the covers and looked at it for a long time as though the limb was that of a strange man behind whose hidden secret being he had arrived.

"But, why was it given to *me* to get behind the poison of life?" he now continued, though only in thought, and stuck his hand under the covers again.

In the living room above him, he heard his boy and girl running hastily, impatiently screaming for something, and behind them came long, laborious steps and a deep voice, frail with age, spoke reassuringly and admonishingly at the same time.

Then the children whirled crashing down the stairs, calling out whilst running, "Goodbye, Therese!", and then slammed the door so that the house shook. Outside they broke out into a laughter which sounded like a childish singsong and then, becoming fainter and fainter, vanished into the distance.

"In any case," Weitfeld resumed his interrupted thoughts, "poison is there. Either in my eyes, in my thoughts, or in Manja's life."

With that he became as still if he had died of horror.

He did not dare move a muscle.

After perhaps an hour, during which he had constantly stared into this turbid darkness, he pulled himself up, tossed the covers off himself and shouted what was held in his throat, "And I should crawl into these fool's rags as if nothing happened and skip about like a clown in them? I, Professor Weitfeld? — That won't happen! Not with my eternal blessing!"

With a shrill laugh of derision, he sank down again, drew the covers over himself and lay, listening tensely to the house, deathly still again like before.

A door was flung open on the upper floor. Mrs Weitfeld's voice called hurriedly and fearfully a few times for old Therese without receiving an answer. Then the Professor's wife came flying down the steps, tore open the door to Weitfeld's bedroom and cried, "For God's sake, what ..." She must have caught sight of the disorder in the room, as she broke off her exclamation, squeezed back out, waited a moment on the threshold and then hesitantly entered again.

"Yes, tell me, I wasn't fooling myself. That was your voice! And here, your clothes? What has happened, sweetheart?" she said with a soft restraint in her voice, remaining standing by the closed door whose handle she was holding.

Weitfeld now sat upright in bed, let his bare, very thin, very hairy legs hang out and looked attentively down at them without answering.

"I have succumbed to an idiosyncracy," he finally said with his old meekness. "Forgive me for frightening you."

Then he lifted his head and looked at her.

"You are already in your painting smock again," he said after that, with a barely noticeable sorrow. "Hmm. Hm. Yes, what you love, you can only do justice to through diligence."

After that he lowered his eyes again to his naked legs and waited for Manja's response.

But Mrs Weitfeld was too bewildered after the wild scream to listen to a perfectly calm man, in the midst of the disorganisation of the orderliness which he loved above all, talking in this way as if he were not sitting in his shirt on the bed, but immaculately dressed at the table and committed to the collected endeavour of creating a meaningful conversation.

For that reason, she remained speechless, let her hand fall from the doorhandle and took an almost inaudible step deeper into the room.

Weitfeld was still sitting bowed on the edge of the bed, but now kept his eyes closed and waited for a response from his wife.

When Manja tried without a sound to help with the continuation of his thought, he opened his eyes a crack, took a furtive half glance at her and interpreted her soundless step into the room as a predisposition to continue the conversation further.

For that reason, he brushed both hands down his blond-haired lower legs and said, "When the poison that Socrates had drunk began to act, his legs began to go cold. But he admonished his friends to sacrifice a chicken to the gods for him."

He spoke quite calmly, more to himself, and laughed, nodding thoughtfully at the same time.

Then he looked at his wife with wide open eyes.

She had turned pale and was staring horrified at him. But her paralysis from fright lasted only a moment. Then she rushed to her husband, shook him by the shoulders and screamed in extreme fear, "Husband, for God's sake, what is it with you? What do you have? What should it mean?"

Weitfeld looked at her calmly, ever smiling, and said, "Don't get excited, Manja. Go and lock the doors. We must speak with one another. What we started yesterday is to be continued. Calm down. I am not Socrates and I have not drunk hemlock. For otherwise I would not have shouted before."

When Manja made no arrangements to comply with his demand, but just watched him timidly, almost in a sort of horror, the Professor rose, walked past her with long, calm strides, locked the doors, withdrew the key, laid it on the bedside cabinet and then returned to his previous place on the edge of the bed.

"You can take the key any moment, unlock the door and leave. I only did it so that we are safe from intrusions. For you know old Therese's way of entering every room unheralded. — — I beg you, Manja, sit yourself down there on the chair. Don't be concerned. I have not taken any poison, that is, not in reality, and I am completely in command of my senses," he said in his accustomed slow way. And since Manja was still standing irresolutely, he repeated somewhat more forcibly, "Yes, please, Manja."

With these almost categorically spoken words, Weitfeld performed with his bare feet a gesture by which he, usually with his hands, reinforced an important wish. He turned the soles of his feet towards one another and fitted the outspread toes exactly to each other. And if that gesture made an amusing impression on the great scholars, it seemed, imitated now by the feet, to be more than comical. Weitfeld, sitting on the edge of the bed, looked no different from an aged ape practising the gestures of climbing on an imagined tree in the desolation of its cage. Hardly had his wife perceived that than, suddenly freed from all apprehensiveness over her husband's incomprehensible conduct, she broke out into the most exuberant laughter and cried, "That is utterly priceless, sweetheart."

Weitfeld raised his sorrowful face and asked with melancholy astonishment, reproachfully and protracted, "So, Manja, what do you mean?"

"Of course," she answered, took off her painting smock, threw it in a great arc over to Weitfeld's clothes on the floor, and concluded, "Certainly, if you want to parley thus, I will undress too and we can make like Adam and Eve."

With that she stepped to the window, opened a pane and tidied her hair to master her excitement. The question passed as a retort through the Professor's head, "*Before* the fall, of course?" But he suppressed the mischief, propped his bent right hand on his thigh and repeated his previous demand, "I beg you, Manja, take a seat."

Despite his indulgent smile, the Professor's face bore the strain of desperate sorrow still deeper, and it seemed somewhat unearthly to Manja again. Thus she drew a chair to the window and, taking her place on it with derisive ceremony, she said mockingly, "God, I'm already sitting. Is this okay, Professor?"

But Weitfeld was no longer paying attention to his wife. He folded his hands, laid them apart, pulled at his fingers and held strained deliberations over in what way he should impart to his wife what was to be said, his head deeply bowed so that his wife, reluctantly bursting out despite the uncertainty of her nature, cried, "This is getting to be absolute nonsense. I don't understand at all why you holler, strew your clothes about the room, and sit half-naked on the edge of the bed like a fakir. It is a right laughable. — Dear. — Weitfeld!! — For God's sake, why did you leave your hat, stick, and overcoat in the doorway of the dining room last night?"

Weitfeld interrupted his deliberations and asked in calm, almost matter-of-fact astonishment, "What, did I do that?"

"Not just that. Boots and socks are also lying on the steps, and how indeed! As if they had fallen from your feet in a wild hurry, one boot on the bottom step, a few steps further a sock and then on the second landing ..."

Weitfeld did not let her finish and said with his face creased with sorrow and a hollow voice, "Yes yes, Manja, I believe it. I believe everything. It is unimaginable otherwise."

"But husband! I, at least, cannot comprehend it!"

Mrs Weitfeld leant back in her chair and covered her eyes with her hand during this anguished exclamation.

"No, that you can't. For that reason as well, I asked you to come to me. It is related — I mean everything that you described — related certainly to the dream in which I lay the entire night.

I want to endeavour to tell it to you.

Bear with me, please.

So, I will see whether I can scrape it together again. I found myself in an immeasurably long train, which was passing through the moonlit night. In full consciousness, I crouched coiled up, stiff, chilled through, in dull apprehensiveness, but at the same time sleeping deeply, in a third class compartment. Around me lay many other men in the same melancholy, lethargic state of sleep; but they were unrecognisable.

I was sitting in my own sleep as though in a glasshouse, noticing everything by me, in me and surrounding me, but was completely self-absorbed."

"Strange," Mrs Weitfeld said.

"Yes, it became even stranger," the Professor agreed with a nod of his head. "Now and then, I heard one of the many fellow passengers groaning out loud from his dream, yet another calling ardently. This one slurring incomprehensibly, that one laughing, and then one screaming out tormentedly.

At the same time, the wheels were stamping in a regular rhythm. From the type of noise, I could make an approximate picture of the nature of the landscape through which we were passing. Sometimes the blustering of the train tailed off gently into the expanses of a great plain, sometimes it resounded back roaring from stone walls, sometimes it darkened near forests into a regular song of ancient basses, something like we once heard in the Alps symphony of Richard Strauss. Do you remember, Manja, that evening at the Philharmonia?"

"I remember. But how did it go on?"

"No, I mean that staging, because of which at the time with the Assessor, Körten, I ..."

"Haha, yes yes. I know. So. It was like a regular song of ancient basses. Enormously interesting."

"No, understand well, Manja. I am thinking of the staging which Nickisch directed and which this Assessor ..."

"But, of course. I know. So, please continue. Like by ancient basses. Gentle, monotonous song. From full leaved, giant tree tops. I understand."

Weitfeld sat there upright and looked at his hands lying pale on his thighs, outstretched, frail and wrinkled. His narration faltered and he did not stir.

When he then raised his head with a jerk and fixed Manja with a sharp look, the colour of her face had turned a paler tone and the lids of her eyes were lowered so that the blue irises were covered by her long, platinum blond eyelashes.

"You see, Manja, it was like that," he said softly, with pained satisfaction in his voice. "But I will continue with my tale. And then the journey rattled shrilly on iron bridges, cracked sometimes like the blasts of a cannon, and then passed again into the eternally empty noise of a barrel-organ. Like it also happens in life. For dreams mirror our existence. And my dream probably also lies in the shadow of my life. —

I travelled and travelled and had the feeling it had already lasted weeks, months, years. The train was endless. An entire people lay sleeping contained within it and were being transported into the unknown. Into another world. Across the borders of existence."

He interrupted himself. For his wife was sitting with a crease in her brow, her head bowed and looking at her interlocked hands, obviously with her thoughts elsewhere.

"Manja," Weitfeld said, "I am telling you my dream."

"Yes, yes. I am listening. Just keep talking," she answered with a soft start, raised her head and looked at him with a mocking smile.

"You know," Weitfeld continued speaking, "and as I thus experienced the entire journey, awake and sleeping at the same time, curled up on the hard bench, shivering, I recognised like lightning that myself and all of us in the train were being transported into chaos. And my apprehensiveness grew to be unbearable.

Finally I couldn't stand it anymore, sprang up and elbowed a path to the window, stepping over the backs and legs of sleeping men and the heads and shoulders of those curled up.

This shaking off of my lethargy, this flaring up out of an all consuming dullness had taken possession like a wildfire of the souls of all the inhabitants of this endless train. As far as I could hear, the noise of awakening men arose in all the wagons. Each wanted at first to be by the window. In silent, dogged hustle, everything became entangled.

Then unexpectedly a metallic rattling broke forth in my wagon, and not only did the windows towards which everything was being shoved come down, but the entire side of the wagon flipped outward with such a sudden jolt that the men forcing towards it could not stop anymore, instead slowly falling out. By some unholy law of that unholy train, whereby nothing was to escape, those toppling out were drawn under the wheels, which raked in the human bodies with almost perverse enjoyment, here a leg, an arm, a head separated, bodies torn up, torsos cut through, in short executing every type of conceivable mutilation on the men.

Meanwhile the opposite side of the wagon had also flipped open, and while the compartment was emptying in this gruesome way on the one side, ever new passengers were climbing on the other side in full motion, their eyes shut, faces pale and still, hypnotised or cataleptic men walking with irresistable, devoted steps past me, and falling like the others under the devouring wheels.

As in our compartment, so it was happening in all the cabins of the endlessly long train, and the railroad embankment and the land next to it were sown with bloodied men shaking with pain, fated to die. No, the entire earth. For in every direction, you could hear the wheezing and stamping of passing trains.

I had up to now been able to hold myself on a protruding beam by utilising all my strength. Finally overwhelmed by horror over so many terrible things, even I weakened. Though I could have held on anyhow for a while more. But one of the men climbing in from the other side, a fattened, blond, unpleasant looking fellow, abandoned his hypersomnia on the way to certain misfortune. He tore his eyes open and looked at me, emitted a wild scream of hate, and threw himself at me all at once. I lost my hold from the impact and, balled up in fury, for I was defending myself desperately, we fell out and ended up like all the others under the wheels."

The Professor had been speaking softer and softer. Now he paused, overwhelmed by the recall of the situation in his dream.

And his wife said, looking rigidly at the floor in front of her, "Gruesome ... ugh ... to dream such a thing!"

But when she raised her head and looked at her husband, her frisson turned into fright. For

Weitfeld was no longer sitting. He was standing, his entire body trembling as though chilled, and looking at her steadily and persistently with a greyish white face and rigid, yet flickering eyes.

At the same time, he repeated almost soundlessly her words, "Gruesome — not so, Manja! Ugh, to dream such a thing! But to live such a thing ... what do you call that? — Hey, Manja?"

He gave the impression of a man over whom madness had taken hold and, after ending his question, lowered his head entirely in the manner of a madman who has overcome an attack, and looked emptily and incuriously at his bare feet. Mrs Weitfeld rose inaudibly and stretched her hand out for the key on the bedside cabinet, so as to escape out of the room with a spring past him.

Weitfeld lifted his eyes and said coldly, "Let the key lie. — I warn you. — We are not yet finished."

And as she was still standing, he added as well, "Sit down and keep listening."

Then, without paying attention to the carrying out of his order, he settled down onto the bed and began rubbing his thigh again. At the same time, he said with a derisive laugh, "The dream is in fact not at an end. If you must know ... hahaha ..."

Then, pausing, he spoke, stooped and pushed on by a clenched chest with a low voice as if he were alone in the room, "By summarising the visible implications, an intellectually understandable, exact differentiation of the events for the purpose of insight into the vital factual circumstances is at least possible. But then the intellectual synthesis never aligns with the synthesis of life, final clarity remains a painful play of mere approximations."

Then he sprang up, wrung his hands and cried painfully begging, "Manja! ... Manja! ... Manja! ..."

Mrs Weitfeld broke out into sobbing tears and covered her face with her hands.

The Professor saw her full, beautiful shoulders shaking and between her fingers swelled the golden yellow locks of her somewhat disordered hair.

He tiptoed to her, drew her hands from her face with restrained force and said, holding them in his own, "Yes, dear woman, it is about life and death with us."

And since she did not answer, but continued crying mutely with lowered face, he let her hands slowly slip away from his grasp again and continued speaking calmly, pursuing the content of the agitation and his dream, "You know, I fell from the carriage and my arm, leg and head were removed from me by the wheels. So that only the trunk remained. But I could not die, not like the other men who had been pulped by the wheels like me. The train carried on and left us mutilated ones behind. But when everything was still in the land, we rose, and as we had lain there, an endless chain of shredded men, so we began a pilgrimage as an endless, unearthly procession through the land, at the same time, the further we advanced, a great fervour took possession of us, and before any of us knew what this feeling in himself meant, everyone was singing enthusiastically, 'Deutschland, Deutschland über alles.'

I, moving myself forward at the end of the bloody troop in a mysterious way, without arms and legs, sang the loudest of all, nevertheless I did not have a head. But from my bloodless arteries, from my wounded heart, my bowels roared and sang it. Every twitching fibre of my deformed trunk had a shrill, but hymnal voice. Even now in waking, it seems to me as if I felt in my body the rhythmic echo of that dreamsong trembling. It was the most terrible thing that I have ever heard, and when I turned around, I noticed that I was not the last of the troop. For behind me came the blond, fattened fellow who had pushed me out of the wagon, fallen with me under the wheels and yet had remained perfectly whole. His mouth flung open so that his impertinent, waxed moustache trembled, he sang like all of us cripples, 'Deutschland, Deutschland über alles.' He sang it lustily, with dancing gait, and the woman who walked by his side and was embraced ardently by him exulted as well and every time the pair's looks fell on my pitiful trunk which could only sing with its bloodless arteries and its half dead, exhausted heart, they broke out into ringing lauhter.

Hahahaha! — Hahahaha ... haha ... haha ... and as I looked closer at who the woman was walking by Körten's side — yes think, the fellow was none other than the Assessor Körten ... by Körten's side, arms interwoven, one with the other, perfectly whole, who this woman was — — — I recognised you ... — Manja! and awoke in fright."

The Professor had been speaking softer and ever softer and had been pushed towards his wife's upper body by the forcefulness of his tale, and now, since he was at the end, he fell silent like after a long run uphill, breathing heavily and with head bent forward, with pale, constricted face and wide-open, penetrating eyes directed at her as though with every fibre of his being, looking like someone jolted out of a deep sleep who has seen something terrible opposite themselves striking at their heart in the dark night and which they cannot recognise. In the room, it was oppressively still like after an explosion.

Manja had stopped her soft sobbing and was staring, with her body bent forward as well, with wide eyes fixed on a mark in the floor.

Then she nodded soundlessly at this mysterious thing she had been looking at, rose with unnaturally quietness and stepped with downcast eyes to the window.

She will dive out, went through Weitfeld's head, who had observed everything surreptitiously and when she just then reached for the window handle as though with detached arms, the Professor sprang behind her, pressed her arms down and said softly with kindhearted reproach, "Manja! Don't!"

She was shaking all over as if with a chill. But now, when he touched her, the fever's spell released her soul. With a scream, she threw her arms around the Professor's neck and then broke out into unfettered sobs.

"Josef ... Weitfeld ... husband, husband ... my God ... oh God. Weitfeld ... my good, dear husband ... I never supposed that you would suffer so ... that you love me so, long for me so ... But my God, how could I even? — I could not know ... if you ... I beg you for all the world, believe me the one ... now, now, at this moment, I know that in my depths I was not unfaithful to you for a second ... never, never ... you golden, best, dearest sweetheart ... will you believe me? ..."

She thus stuttered incoherently between the bouts of crying, sometimes in despair, sometimes in exultation, flinging her arms around her husband's neck, letting him go, walking a little way into the room with outstretched arms, sitting down, springing up, in short, ceded herself to the whirl of feeling of someone saved who, after a long time in darkness, enthuses without restraint over the light and would rather carry the colour of dislocation and morbid exuberance on herself than the shimmer of joyous transfiguration.

Weitfeld had embraced his wife carefully on the first outpouring, and endeavoured to lead her away from the window to the chair.

But when his delighted wife fell on him like a spring storm, almost suffocated him with kisses, let him go, swept through the room and fell on his neck again, he realised there was no need to be frightened for her life, gave up his endeavours around her, and began to collect his clothes together and get dressed. He undertook this business matter-of-factly with constricted, bitter attentiveness and listened meanwhile to Manja's enthusing, self-accusations, exultation, and sorrow as they drove her through the room, pressed her now and again into her chair and then led her again to his chest.

Everything which had been amassing in her heart secretly for years was freed by the flooding and fell foaming and disordered like backwaters from her, "You see, I tell you, if you had not flipped your lid to leave Berlin on the spot, to abandon your chair, your career, your fame, your whole life ..."

Weitfeld, who had just been about to lift his vest from the floor, threw it reluctantly back down on the floor and murmured reluctantly, "Oh what academic career and fame. Simply ridiculous ..."

"But now, sweetheart ... It is wonderful that everything seems unimportant to you before the fact of aggrieved love ... wonderful, I am happy ... Josef, Josef, God, my Seppi ..."

Manja glowed, embraced her husband again, nestled like a sucking, blazing flame in him, so that the pulses of fire also awoke in the tall, gaunt, wrinkled man. He certainly clenched his teeth in defence; but his wife sensed how she was being embraced by his arms ever more passionately and powerfully, and she lisped greedily, "... dear Seppi ... my sole beloved husband ... believe me, not the smallest thing happened between me and Körten ... Seppi ... Seppi ..., you know, because you did not take care of me at all, I sent him the pictures, we exchanged letters, and all openly with the assistance of Griepenstein, everything oiled to get your shackles up, to wound you, to needle you. But you sleep calmly up here, and I over there, you let your fame decay, meditate, make mushroom magic, act like a wooden idol ... I was desperate, Seppi ... I did not know ... God, thank God, sweetheart ... Seppi, take me! —"

On the way to the bed, the woman said all that passionately, as though under a hot torch, no longer in control of herself after years of being deprived of every tenderness.

The Professor was breathing fitfully and was already having to make forceful swallowing motions.

"... Just be quiet, Manja ... calm down ..." he whispered with the barking voice of a man who is on the point of being seared by the fire of sex. The play of colours was also starting before his eyes as they closed for the sleep of ecstasy. Wheels of light were dancing, red arrows darted through the blackness.

Only, suddenly he plunged with the aeroplane of his eroticism out of the blazing sky, for in the swarm of chasing colours, his circle with the inscribed pentagon and triangle stood before him in the universal primary colours of green, blue and brown. He was as if nailed down in his innermost being and something, even bitterer than scorn was originating from it.

Then his grasp on his hotly melting wife unfastened itself and, with superhuman effort, he straightened up palely before his startled wife, who looked at him flustered and shook her head.

Struggling for poise, he said softly and humbly ashamed, "No, Manja, forgive me, I truly don't want to say it. It isn't about this with me. No. Really. Forgive me. Please, give me your hand."

With that he led the woman startled out of all heavens to her chair.

Then he took a few steps away from her, turned away, covered his eyes with his hands and waited a long while thus without stirring, in self-absorption and silence. When he finally turned around, his wife sat half turned away on the chair and had buried her head in her arms propped on the back rest. Weitfeld thought that the high swing of disillusionment by which he had been seized and forced unopposed into meditation had now been transferred to Manja telepathically and with happy, almost timid pity, he said, "Manja — dear ... oh, you are still sunk in thought. Forgive me!"

And hastily and entirely without a sound, he completed getting dressed.

But his wife remained motionless in her averted self-absorption.

Then he stroked the ridge of his nose a few times with two fingers, brooding, paused to consider, threw a long, wide-eyed, hypnotic look at her, and when that did not help awaken her, he traced her image in the air with his hands a few times, starting from her head.

But Manja lay in the night of her bitter, feminine shame, in a consuming paralysis, numbed, and the blood was roaring through her temples.

In his socks, the Professor now came a few steps closer, indecisively and inaudibly, but then paused and began softly to speak, softly and sparingly like you tend to speak to someone who has just awoken, "You see, Manja, now the gates have also opened for you, the gates through which it led me years ago. It was hard. But it has succeeded. Praise God. Stay resting in bed. I know that. All deep knowledge begins with deep numbing.

Let me help the blossoming of your soul. But don't force yourself to listen. As soon as it fills you with indignation, you may just give me a silent signal and I will fall silent and pull back."

He waited and watched his wife's shoulders and head attentively for whether a repulsing movement was rising in them.

Manja lay motionless, bent over the back of the chair. Weitfeld sat down soundlessly on a chair somewhat away from her, still watching her a little for the most exact movement and then nodded contentedly.

"Yes, stay like that," he said, "it is at least an adequate, productive pose. The predominance of the spiritual, of the sense of hearing, will thereby unburden you. The field of vision vanishes into the horizonless spiritual apperception. Respectively ... but that is incidental. So, to clear away a misunderstanding first, it must be said that the entanglements of an opinion are to be dissolved, those that appear more deeply decayed to you than those I myself suffered under last night in my dream and yesterday afternoon. I mean the fact of the delusion of my jealousy for this Assessor Körten for whom you have soothed his urging in your being by a willingness which from your side was only played with concern for its stimulating effect on me.

Have I understood you thus correctly?"

The Professor saw a jolt pass through his wife's body, as if she wanted to rise to a passionate rejoinder. But it remained at a short rising up. In the next moment, she lay even more motionless, more like a frail, torn perennial, and he could not see the breath shaking her back anymore.

Weitfeld took this gesture from his despairing wife as affirmation of his question, and hence continued, "Good. That is how the matter lies. Now, however, you always end up in irresolvable entanglements when you seek to answer a question according to the purely subjective conditions. For the individual is just as much anarchy as mechanical system. And if we look at humanity as a whole, we notice that the conditions on earth certainly remain continually the *same*, even if the modality of their forms is infinite.

The type of existence does not change within the epochs. The generic characteristics are stable. They come with the being into the world, which must not be proud of them, for that is not its subjective property. I know that I stand thereby in abrupt opposition to the teachings of evolution. But that I don't contest. I have seen through it as the human utilitarian principle practised in the cosmic, grandiose manner, which we project forcibly onto the universe.

Despite all this rhetoric, the crow remains just the crow, it turns its head, today just like a hundred thousand years ago, to the right and to the left, flaps its wings, peers with head askew, sometimes into the sky, sometimes at the manure heap on which we both observed it yesterday.

It would be foolishness to quarrel over it.

And even people live and die mostly in the cage of the class and gender in which they were born. The living are always pulling on the discarded clothes of the dead, and to the tailor, Harun al Raschid and the emperor Wilhelm II are one and the same figure.

But, my dear Manja, this mechanical system which goes through the millenia like a dreary, straight, monotonous flight, it comprehends also, just as in itself, the relationship of genders to one another, thus the relationship between husband and wife.

Generally speaking, you describe this side of the cosmic mechanism, to which low-minded men are subject, as divine.

But all that is physical is just emanation of the spiritual, and expression of its inner state of form. This cannot on the other hand be valued or treasured by itself, but only by a higher instance, the soul.

Hence we are in the realm of divine anarchy, in the area of aimless knowledge, on the other side of all mundane individual barriers. Anyone who arrives in this expanse, finds himself on the other side of the mechanical compulsion of all modalities, thus even of the modality of sex, and will grant a right to themselves as a spiritual counterpart, which is certainly a form, but never the objective in itself."

Weitfeld had immersed himself unawares in the hot, subterranean waves by which his life had been carried for years. It had driven him from his chair and, sometimes staring at the floor in front of him, sometimes lifting his eyes up out of the boundless, he walked excitedly with his long, dipping stride back and forth in the narrow space of the room.

He had so busied himself with his ideas that he had stopped observing the impression of his words on Manja. Now, heading back on his passionate walk, he saw she was no longer in the pose of deep meditation half turned away on her arms lying across the back of the chair, but instead he found her in passionate excitement, no, in a sort of dogged numbness, sitting upright almost on the edge of the chair, her feet drawn back as if ready to spring, her hands clasped as wildly in her lap as if she were someone fallen from a great height, holding desperately to a rope, and just as wildly resolute was the expression on her discoloured, hollowed face.

Weitfeld saw in this pose the expression of her emotion over his clarification. He had often experienced it with his most devoted listeners in the auditorium and dubbed it bewilderment of cognition. When the shock to the spirit of the others had succeeded to this level, it needed even less effort to achieve perfectly the victory of a new thesis.

So he remained standing, looked contentedly at his shaken wife, raised his hand triumphantly and cried, "Yes, yes, dear Manja, it stands thus and no differently before the eyes of the highly confused: you must hold yourself to be too good for the coarse sex drive to strike out its few ancient, brutal chords from our being."

At this outburst, Manja undid the entanglement of her hands, embraced her knees as though in an unnaturally anguished feeling of pain, raised her face and looked at him completely flustered.

Then she moved her head in disagreement and sighed a few times, "No ... no ..."

"Yes, Manja," Weitfeld cried protesting, "yes, I tell you. If you want, feel it! Convince yourself for my sake manually. Even the last breath has vanished from my sex drive."

With an anguished cry, his wife let her upper body sink down slowly and hid her face in her hands.

"Terrible ... terrible ..." she murmured at the same time and shivered.

"Oh no, not terrible, not terrible," the Professor cried seemingly ecstatic, "glorious, dear Manja, glorious, I tell you. We stand *above* everyone thereby. Now really two people who deserve the privilege of being called *homo sapiens* indeed. I, as far as I am a husband, am to you, in so far as you are a wife, from now on guilty of nothing anymore and vice versa. With this base, brutal instance, we are finally finished. With that, we have nothing more to create from now on. We are divine. For not a shimmer of the sexual nexus reaches to the soul and God."

After this new outburst, Manja raised her upper body slowly and stiffly. Her face was strange and calm. She did not look at her husband, but kept looking past him, unerringly towards the corner of the room.

"And your walk yesterday afternoon to the porter Käse and to Malva Griepenstein?" she asked firmly.

"I admit, a last atavistic mood."

"And this wild night with the wild dream and your screaming this morning?" she continued steadfastly.

"Yes, what do you want from that then? About this fact, we are long past caring, Manja! — On Goethe's second Swiss journey, an explanation of the sort occurred of how mules take rugged slopes. They run quickly forwards, then suddenly stop and often indeed in the most dangerous spot ..."

Manja curved her lips into a mocking smile and interrupted him, "Well and good. And so you did not leave Berlin in 1915 because of *me* either. That is, *not* from jealousy over Körten?"

"No, haha, God knows, at base not because of that superficial doctor of nothing. Haha! No, I'd had enough of life among my colleagues, among these hucksters of the so-called sciences."

"That is now three years ago?" she asked ever more firmly and muter.

"Yes, quite right, three years, agreed," Weitfeld answered, becoming uncertain. "Manja, I beg you ..." But she did not let him finish.

"Ten years our marriage has lasted," she continued with a chill in her voice, paused for a moment as though pining, and then finished tormentedly, "And three years apart. Three *entire — full — long* years."

At the same time, she rose from her seat without turning her eyes away from the corner of the room.

"And that shall continue for year after year. Year after year. Until death."

"But dear Manja, just listen," Weitfeld cried insistently and yet also aroused by a fear. "*Not* grey, *not* empty, *not* uneventful. No, in contrast. Don't you see it then? The communion of bodies is now overcome. The highest, divine form of marriage begins now. Henceforward it is okay, on the basis of individual deepening, to achieve a higher, spiritual unity under the obliteration of the cerebral mycelium of the topsoil of spiritual energy by differentiation and the potentialisation of our personality."

Then strength deserted the brave, dear woman. She began to stagger, grasped at the back of the chair and sank to her knees by the chair, burying her face in her hands again.

Weitfeld still did not understand her in his fanatical blindness.

"Yes, dearest wife," he cried rapturously, "you are right. It is to stagger, to fall on your knees. Oh, and our children first! Manja, what is to us the end and the highest, shall be a valley to them. They shall wear garments in their adulthood, dear, dearest wife, garments of which you and I know nothing at all. Then there will be no human hate anymore on earth, no war, no curse of national hostilities ..."

Manja had begun sobbing. Despite her resisting, it swelled up. With her hands balled up into fists, she pressed her handkerchief to her mouth. But the crying swelled into convulsions. Her body was shaken by bouts of despairing sobs and she stuttered screaming, "But ... husband ... hus ... ba ... and ... listen though ..."

"You're always crying, dearest. From our anguish, from our struggle, the new world is being born," he cried in a wild rapture. Then he stepped up to her, bent down and asked, "What is it? What are you saying? I don't understand you."

Then his wife became deathly still all at once. The world became a transparent coffin and you could again hear nothing but the summer flies pecking helplessly at the panes.

In this deathly silence, his wife, her face pressed firmly on the cane of the chair's seat, spoke softly and with shudders, "I have been with Körten once already and have lost myself in him. Husband!! — Husband!!"

Weitfeld drew back the hand he had placed comfortingly on her shoulder, took a step away from her and looked for a moment at his cupped hand taken aback. This hesitation lasted only a moment. Then his old intoxication flew over him. He stepped vehemently up to her, seized her by the shoulders, and in his effort to lift her up, he spoke to her aghast, "But let that be. That belongs to your old, deceased life. I am not grieving over that. It is waived. Now the current of the soul is pushing ..."

But with a scream of horror, his wife tore herself away from him, dealt him a blow to the chest with her fist so that he staggered back, and hurled in his face the exclamation, "Ugh! Ugh!!"

Then she gathered the key from the bedside cabinet, stormed through the door, and slammed it behind her.

6

With excessive enjoyment of alcohol, drinkers pass through inebriation into the second state of intoxication, into a dazzling, almost hectic, excessive clarity of thought, into a state in which the last shadow of sympathy and partisanship also vanishes with the motions of their deliberation towards themselves.

Such a thing was happening to Professor Weitfeld in the first moments after his wife had left him and he saw himself all alone in the room, fallen from the peak of his highest rapture.

The entire house had been suddenly killed by the blast with which Manja had thrown the door shut behind her, as though shot through the middle of the heart, and he was standing in the breathless silence of a morgue without comprehending how everything had come and gone. He heard her steps flying up the stairs, stumbling in the hall up above, picking herself up, scurrying on and vanishing behind another slamming door as though with an explosion.

At that he touched with his hand the middle of his chest where his wife's blow had struck, nodded to himself gravely and as if in acknowledgement, and then carried the chair by which Manja had been kneeling crying into the darkest corner of the room. The handkerchief which she had let fall on the ground, torn up in the convulsions of despairing sobs, he did not touch. "May it remain lying as *corpus delicti*. For if I bring her attention tomorrow to her exaltation, she will want to have no word of it again. And everything would again be nothing but 'senile reclusive rubbish from me'," he spoke softly to himself as he returned from the corner of his room to the middle and he smiled derisively with a pale face and endless bitterness. Thus he surveyed his large room in a sort of helpless arrogance, as if he were standing in a desert with the endless, darkening horizon on all sides.

And with all this bitter, derisive, arrogant calm, a wild, terrible, no, a bestial scream lay in his throat, against whose outburst he fought arduously, because he felt certain that he would have to then spring first of all at the closed door with his fists and feet, smash it in, and then be forced to rampage like a madman in the house, to run into the street, to set the entire village in turmoil, "to annihilate the entire damned, tainted world of lustful human dogs — to annihilate — annihilate ..."

Without knowing it, his thoughts had become loud words whose echo he, abruptly startled no less than if he were falling for a stretch through the air, now heard resounding in the room, and he found himself breathing as though seething, staring at the door with balled fists.

He shook his head with a disapproving smile over his "inner unfetteredness" and brushed his right hand from his forehead down over his face, wiping away the strain of a nasty cramp.

"It is ridiculous," he said at the same time in a sudden outbreak of cheerfulness, "total nonsense to work myself up like that."

But then he noticed his wife's painting smock on the floor and at once the wildness broke forth again, "This damned, damned painting smock is still lying here too and she knows that disorder can make me mad."

Weitfeld bore down on the piece of clothing, lifted it up, threw it against the floor so that the buttons clattered, kicked it with his feet and shouted constantly, "Such smut! Such damned smut, I will not tolerate ... not tolerate ... I will not tolerate it ... un...der ... any ... cir...cum... stances..."

He pushed Manja's painting smock across the entire room with his feet until it had been kicked under his bed.

He was staggering with rage so that he had to support himself with his hand on the bedside cabinet.

Then he stretched out his hand, looked at his palm for a long time attentively and, forcing him- self into his old meekness with all his might, murmured softly, almost tearfully kindhearted, "That ... that won't work ... Weitfeld ... no ... no ..."

But he had to interrupt the indecisive thoughts of the appeasement which he wanted to work his way towards, for he heard outside in the hallway the cautious steps of men approaching his door, looked down at himself, noticed he was still in his socks and listened with a little anxiety for whether there would be a knock on the door. Then he would go into his study on tiptoe and soundlessly draw the door shut behind himself.

But the knock remained undone.

After he had waited a moment yet and had reached the conviction that nobody was standing outside, he fetched his shoes from the threshold, sat on the chair by his bed, on which he tended to leave his clothes, and began to put them on, bending down, an impractical habit which he had kept since his boyhood. That is, he did not place his shoe on the chair to lace it up, but managed the business in a much more cumbersome way, in that he, bending down to the floor, hastily wound the laces through the eyelets after he had drawn the shoes onto his feet. When he had finished the work on his right foot, he had to straighten up his bent posture, for he had an attack of dizziness. Yes, even when he had been sitting down with straightened upper body and eyes shut for a while, the entire room was still swaying and flittering around him.

"This is an unusual state of bother," the Professor thought, "this entire ball of undealt-with half-truths in which I am entangled because I have engaged again in this delusion of the relativity of thought."

With that he opened his eyes again to discover whether the congestion had fallen away.

Yes, now everything was right again. The pattern of the wallpaper was unmistakable on its greyish blue background. None of the dark little points were stirring anymore. The portiere before the door into his study was hanging motionless again. Next to it, on the etching by Aust, "The Landeck Biele Bridge", he saw clearly the blessed Nepomuk enthroned on the wall enclosure of the bridge.

But, as he was examining things in this way and he moved his gaze further to the left, coming upon the dark corner in which he had previously placed Manja's chair, he had to look away and close his eyes again.

A field grey man was sitting there on the chair in his coat, his legs thrown apart, with a provocatively erect upper body and his bent right hand propped on his knee.

"A self-deception," Weitfeld thought and remained with eyes shut for a while.

"Open your eyes, Professor," a voice spoke to him, its polite tone sounding derisively mocking.

Weitfeld started now in fright, but recalled having read that auditory delusions could also happen with waking deceptions, placed his right hand over his eyes, leant back on the chair and decided to let the attack pass in peace.

But then the voice began speaking again, "Professor, you treated your adored wife, who has been thus adored for the longest time, in the lowest, most base manner before. You possessed the sombre courage for it. Yes. But now, since I have arrived to demand satisfaction for it from you, you cover your eyes in a cowardly manner, and act as if I am an apparition."

It was unmistakably the pretentiously purring organ of the Assessor Körten which he was hearing then.

"To hell with everything," it rose up furiously in Weitfeld as if the voice and the image were not the ghost of his overwrought being, but really his wife's hated lover who, in an incomprehensible way, had slipped into the room behind him when he had pulled his shoes in from the threshold.

The Professor splayed the fingers of the hand with which he had covered his eyes a bit and peered through the gaps to see whether the figure was still present on the chair.

The Assessor was sitting there in the same pose, yet more provocatively than before. "It is pure nonsense in the light of day," Weitfeld murmured. "I slept badly, add to that my upsetting conversation with Manja and my empty stomach. That is all."

With that he rose, turned his back on the pernicious corner, placed his left foot on the chair and began to lace up the other shoe. He had barely started with that when the Assessor behind him began talking to him again, but now with such a wounding scorn that, already after the first words, it took Weitfeld's breath away in fury.

"Haha! Ridiculous! You turn away. Thus you, sir, prefer to turn inwardly. Leave this imposture of internationalism, this hokus pokus with the higher character of humanity. Put real German boots on your feet and march away. You make yourself and the entire nation ridiculous in this way.

What sort of juice for sucklings is that which you have brewed together here in Johnsbach?

For spitting! — And because of this lollipop, you gave up your chair. You, the hope and pride of German philology, you, the author of the epochal, three volume work 'The Valley of Languages'."

"Thunderbolts!" Weitfeld shouted in extreme agitation, jumped up, seized the chair with both hands by the backrest and heaved it at the floor so it thundered. Then he took long strides to the door of his study without throwing a glance at the chair, but yet so gravely and scornfully that it could not remain without effect if the utterly inconceivable thing, that this Körten had slipped in behind his back and was sitting there, were nevertheless fact.

The Professor parted the portiere and disappeared into his study.

"Such nonsense! Such dementedness," he murmured in flight, almost breathless. "And it has to happen to me? To me! I have to wallow in this excrement! Do I?"

He immediately began pacing about his writing table with feverish haste. "I know that everything is over. She also ought to have. With skin and hair, she ought to have ... with skin and hair. — Thank God that it has happened thus. Yes. I had an angel so to speak. Since yesterday morning. Since the crow. Blessed bird. Truly! — What deep symbolism, it sitting on the manure heap. — Yes, really prophetic. — Everything on which I built is now mouldy — ... mouldy ... rubbish ..."

He sat down at his writing table and continued saying just those last two words. His elbows propped on the armrests, his head turned to the floor, he memorised the breakdown of his existence whilst speaking just the two words ever slower and softer. Without knowing what was happening to himself, the tears ran down his cheeks.

Then he sank into silent brooding.

7

The staring lead almost wrenchingly into sleep, like falling water plunging into a pool. Resting on his arms, his mouth wide open as though in a dying scream, his hands soaked in the drool of fatigue, he slept.

The midday bells did not wake him; the rampaging return home of his children did not stir him. The maidservant knocked. First little Georg came, pecked abruptly and ever harder on the door and cried out, "Papa, come and eat! Mama gives her apologies. She has a migraine, papa!" Then, when he received no answer and had hurried off to his sister, the children even dared to open the door a crack and whisper their little statute timidly through it.

When they saw their father thrown motionless over the table the way the dead sleep, they ran in delirious terror to old Therese and reported that their father was sitting below and had died, for he was not breathing like a man, but merely like a machine.

Therese, the old, dear house fixture, dried her hands on her apron, conveyed them, bravey smiling, into the dining room to their plates and then climbed with shaking head and bitter smile down to the lower floor.

Her cautious knocking, her careful entry, it was all no help. The Professor lay as though decapitated on his arms, his mouth wide open in a scream, the drool running from his lips, and when the old woman finally dared to lay her hand delicately on his shoulder and to whisper, "Come, Professor. Or at least go to bed," the sleeping man's face blanched even more, distorted itself in despairing grief, and a soft groan, from the depths of his chest, struggled from his mouth with incomprehensible words. Then Therese noted well that a fate was being composed right there. She drew back carefully from the deeply aggrieved man and shut the door without a sound.

Weitfeld continued to sleep, hour after hour. Towards four o'clock in the afternoon, his breathing became easier. The expression of despairing grief vanished from his face. His mouth closed.

Finally he straightened up, saw the drool on his hands, wiped it off with his handkerchief, looked around his room as though in a strange place, shook his head, laid the fingertips of both hands on each other, and then rose with an abrupt jerk, like he was drowsy, stepped into his bedroom and looked to the chair in the dark corner where the Assessor Körten had been sitting before. It was empty.

Remaining silent, Weitfeld shut the door and stepped back into his room.

Quite high in the infinity above him, he heard something like the clamour of wings tearing past, endless flocks of birds.

"The crows. Always the crows," he murmured aggrieved and bewildered.

Then he sat down at his writing table, took a thick, well-thumbed book bound in rough linen and buttoned up above and below with ribbons of the same material, opened it up and began after a short meditation to inscribe the following, "All of us who have become grey in brooding know finally about the relativity of the final, logically clearly comprehensible reasons, and can and must not let it nevertheless be left to drive us in circles from causality. For as long as men live whose hearts cannot be plundered by the wind like caraway flowers in the field, but, like a precious bell in a secret place, can only be brought to ring by a purified hand — by our, our purest hand — as long as such lean and affluent, such victoriously destroyed, destroying men live under the sun, they will always go like Saint Augustine to the shore of the sea and attempt with obstinacy to master for the world the ocean of worldly mysterious fortune with the little narrow hand of their days."

Then he struck out the last verb and wrote in its place the word "rescue", was not even content with that, placed the pen down, and murmured at the same time, "No, it's not working!" and propped his head in both hands for a moment.

After a little thought, he reached for the pen again, ripped a passionate stroke under what he had written and began to inscribe the following in his diary, "All men surely have the intuition that they are bound with the others in a deeper, spiritual way than that of trade and business, of basic needs and utility, but admit to it only the narrow circle of their close friends, and with those people to which they feel chained by a deep fervour of love or hate. On whatever powers of their deepest nature this universal connectivity of souls is based, almost everyone resists their response to this knowledge from the very correct feeling that then the randomness and disconnectedness of their accustomed moral conduct would be made impossible for them. And so they content themselves with being astonished pleasantly or frightfully over wondrous infatuations of the senses, curious dreams and strange shifts of mood, or just calm themselves as educated men with Hamlet. But even deeper, graver natures notice on this side of life only rarely the thousandfold forms of human existence which are connected in all directions so that they also teach the great, serene spirits the feeling of the infinity of mundane life forms."

Weitfeld had been writing ever slower and more petulantly. Now he put the pen aside and murmured bored, "Oh, what use is it still?"

Then he shoved the book across the desk, lay on his arms and, after a few seconds, had again fallen into the death-like sleep.

Towards evening he awoke with a start as though wildly shaken. The sky had reddened softly like an eye that has stared too long into the glaring light.

Weitfeld sprang from the chair, stepped to the window, threw a quick look outside, returned to his desk, read over what he had written, laughed derisively, tore the pages from the book, and stuffed them in his sidepocket with the words, "Nonsense! Rubbish! It's past. Yes, yes, my Körten, now *we* are marching."

After that, he paced through his room a few times. The seesawing dipping had vanished completely from his gait. He walked with quick skips and his face had that expression peculiar to fanatical ascetics. With a jolt, he suddenly broke off the stalking before the door to his bedroom.

"An end to it! An end to it!" he cried with angry resolve.

Then he took all the money from his writing desk, pocketed it, and went with long strides hurriedly into the bedroom. He came out of it after a short period in half stockings and sport coat, with a fully packed rucksack over his shoulders.

On the upper floor, he encountered Therese just coming out of the kitchen.

"Where is my dear wife?" he asked calmly.

"Locked in her room," she answered timidly and startled because of his pale face and his rigid, yet blazing eyes.

"Good," he said. "Go into the dining room. I have something to tell you. The children should be there too. But immediately."

Then he remained standing and drew something on the floor with his stick.

Therese called the children from their room and went with them upset into the dining room.

When the hallway was calm, Weitfeld fetched a deep breath, stepped to the door of his wife's room, knocked hard and when the call from within came, "Who's there?", he said with shaking voice, "Manja, open up."

"No, never," his wife called swiftly, but with turgid, misshapen voice, "never! You are not a husband anymore. You are just a procurer of the spirit, a ... a ..." The rest sank into anguished crying, all the rest, which sounded like a single long invective. Weitfeld bit his lip and looked at the floor. When it had turned quiet within, he looked down the hall, bent his head close to the door and said, "Now. I wanted to announce to you that you are free for ever. Live as well as you can. Since you are not going *with* me, I must go *without* you. Farewell, Manja!"

Then he waited for a moment longer.

It remained still in the room and Weitfeld stepped slowly over to the dining room.

There both his children were sitting timidly on chairs and looking helplessly and scared at their father who paused in the doorway on entering and embraced them with his eyes for a long time. The children lowered their heads before his look.

When Weitfeld noticed that, he nodded in bitter thought and slowly brushed his hand over his forehead.

"Yes," he then said as though awakening from a long, difficult dream. "You know, Jörg and Sissi. I must go into the mountains. I am overworked and must be alone. Obey your mother well and always be nice. Don't forget me completely either. Farewell — for the time being. I must see that I get going. Before the night falls, I must be up there. Farewell, farewell, children." With that he embraced them as if he wanted to crush them and kissed them fervently while they let it all happen as though paralysed.

When he stepped away from them, they laid their arms on the table and began crying softly.

Weitfeld signalled to Therese with his eyes and she followed him into the hall.

There he stood and looked at the old woman for a while deliberating, scrutinising, perhaps with a little dithering of his resolve in his face.

"You know, Therese," he then said softly and slowly, but laughed aloud suddenly.

"Oh, well! Farewell and take care," he cried exuberantly, pressed her hand and *skipped* primly down the stairs, hurried through the garden, and had soon disappeared.

When Therese awoke from her paralysis and realised what had happened, she ran down the stairs after him and shouted primly, "Professor! — Professor!"

But the garden was empty. The little gate stood open, and nothing was to be seen of him but the traces of his steps in the sand.

8

When the Professor had aproached the edge of the village with quick steps and, after crossing the main road, had entered the sloping terrain of the meadows which rose quickly towards the foothills, it was already that greatest time of evening beauty in which sometimes the whole land up to the feet of the Sudeten Mountains was still lit by that shimmer which was made unreal by their transfiguration. Like a magical, supernatural exaltation, they smouldered garishly and glassily behind a reddish haze which nevertheless did not seem like the refraction of the sun, already sunk behind the high mountains, but like the breath of the mountain range itself, which showed itself for once in its autonomous beauty, whereas it usually always lived by the grace of the day star.

When this magic of the heights occurred, Weitfeld paused on the narrow path which he had set foot on, as if stopping on a call from out of the air, plunged on with fervent looks into this thousand coloured phantasmagoria above him, swung his stick with an almost jubilant wildness over his head, and cried aloud as though saved, "Yes! Yes! Now up and at it."

A few woodcutters, who were climbing with staves on their shoulders down an adjoining path out of the forest, looked over to him, exchanged a few mocking remarks and then separated, each heading for a different wooden hut which lay hidden amidst a few fruit trees. Weitfeld paid no attention to them, but resumed his flight with long, avid steps. He had soon disappeared into the forest over the Mathilde heights and, barely three quarters of an hour later, he entered the small, meadowy high plateau in which the little village of Wiesenfeld tailed off towards the high mountains.

Without resting and already in the dusk and the pale ghosting of the rising full moon, he passed over the small plain enclosed by forest, entered the steep path, and then stormed irresistably to the crest in the region of the great snow cirques.

With that the track actually died out for a long time, I mean the certain tracks of this famed academic into the Sudeten Mountains. With his entrance into the high forest that evening, he vanished, though not from the earth. But it cannot be untangled as to how many inner and outer transformations, obscurities and contortions burdened, darkened and disfigured him until the point in time in which he publicly emerged into the garish glow of wild, unshackled events and for weeks drew the attention of all Germany to himself. But it is certainly not right to set against him all the malign, passionately spiteful revelations and malicious exposés about the existence and life habits of Weitfeld, with which the Professor's bare-of-all-means and abandoned wife went to market everywhere as it were; it is not true that he, barely having stepped out of the house, mingled among a swarm of workers who were coming from the nearby paper factory to heat up their already present political radicalism even more by provocative talk, yes to spur them on to the direct path to active resistance against the endless resumption of the senseless bloodshed. The working classes of this populous and industrially rich mountain village always stood on-call for bold obstructiveness. It is a fact that on this night in which Professor Weitfeld's flight from his house and former life took place, a Sunday evening towards the end of August 1918, in the vicinity of the Blue Helmet tavern, a wild jeering, shouting and whistling arose. With the cry, "Strike him dead, the war profiteer and oppressor of men," a heap of mostly young workmen poured into the lanes in front of the houses of the genteel and rich. Everywhere the gangs howled the same slogan, "Down with the war!" and then began bombarding the windows and doors with stones. The gendarme who rushed there was trounced, someone broke his bayonet, snatched his revolver from him before he could shoot, smashed the weapon useless, jeering, threw it in the Zacken and conveyed the poor security man over the high wall on the banks of the Zacken and straight into the deepest place, so that he limped out again like a drowned rat. But with the plopping slam of his body into the mirrored waters, the clamour and uproar was cut off abruptly and, in the dark of midnight, the founders of the unrest had vanished as if from the earth.

The dirtied gendarme now maintained that the leaders of the rioters had been two soldiers from the border police who had not actually returned to their quarters on this day but vanished without trace.

It was these same soldiers who on the same day after the relief of their posts on the ridge, somewhat after ten o'clock at night, had demanded entry with shouts and baton strikes on the door to the Big Lime Tree tavern in Wiesenfeld. The owner of the premises had fallen in Russia two years before and his only son was in the Crown Prince's army by Verdun. So the widow was running the business alone with her only daughter and a maid. When she heard the urging of the men, which seemed more like a heist by robbers, the three feminine beings agreed to still give some resistance, to attempt to move the excited men to go away amicably, and above all to scout out who they were and what they wanted.

The sleek maid undertook the negotiations with the men, and it was soon revealed that it was the two staid Bavarians who, day after day, sometimes on the way to the crest, sometimes on the return from service in the mountains, always stopped off for a while at the Lime Tree and offered everyone an enjoyable sport with their grumbling good nature and their honest fury over the "sacrilegiously damned sour beer". Hardly had the maid discovered who the two robbers were than she opened the door for them laughing, because she was certain of soon joshing the two excited men again into their old grumbly grinning. Only, she was mistaken. The soldiers did not behave like drunks, no, more like madmen, lunatics excited to the extreme, and immediately began a threatening gibberish about "the power of men", "the nonsense of all powers and all kings", "the curse of war" and much more even, banged on the tables with their bayonets, and immediately requested wine and food, as much as was in the house, otherwise they would smash "the entire pile of rubbish" to bits and whoever made a move to resist would, by God, be immediately eliminated. After that, they were sometime waving about with knives, sometimes messing about with the rifles. The maid soon had to realise that nothing was working with her archness, and dragged out in fear everything that the raving men demanded. From the dark corner next to the door, she meanwhile paid attention to their conversation, in which again and again "the coral stones", a group of rocks halfway up to the crest, and a tall, "educated" gentleman played a role. That was all. The common people had to take things into their own hands. Not before all the old order had been destroyed could the new man be thought of in the new realm, the two men made such and similar talk, laughing loudly in between, drinking to each other, cheering each other mutually, stomping back and forth without paying any attention to the maid and the bill, with the assurance of starting that very day with the knocking over of the whole lot. Before the door, one of them turned around and instilled in the girl that nobody was to betray anything of what had happened there, otherwise they would come again and make "the entire mob a head shorter." In the garden, they smashed their rifles to bits on a tree and then ran down the mountain to Johnsbach so that the stones of the path rolled after their steps.

Around the middle of the same night, the tumult in Johnsbach broke out and when the Chief Superintendent of this place had received knowledge of the events in the Lime Tree tavern, he formed the conviction that a foreign agitator had undermined the attitudes of the border soldiers and, immediately after, the compelling suspicion arose that this founder of unrest was none other than Professor Weitfeld, who had been behaving strangely for a long time, had expressed to the

Consul Griepenstein and other persons captious and directly subversive views, and had abandoned his wife. By her voluntary testimony over his ideas, which spoke scorn on everything that not only the Germans, but every man held for sacred, it became completely certain that it had been none other than Weitfeld who, in the night at the coral stones, had talked the border soldiers into public revolt and desertion.

So as not to scare gentle folk to their depths yet more, and so as not to help the hidden blaze in many a breast break out, the Chief Superintendent hushed up the nocturnal fuss as much as possible and ascribed it to a childish desire for a racket by boyish louts. On the quiet, he continued the vigilance over the escaped Professor and induced the commander of the border police to a strengthened patrol after the supposed malefactor on the entire crest, starting from Schmiedeberg and going all the way to the depression behind Reifträger. But he was not found, although it was certain that Weitfeld had still been in the mountains in the following days.

For the landlord of the snow cirques' inn had heard on the day after the Johnsbach tumult, towards morning, but still in darkness, stumbling steps around the building like the gait of an exhausted man, and was about to get up to fetch the passerby in. But soon after the person began speaking, as it seemed to him, sometimes in a high, sometimes in a deep man's voice, sometimes near, sometimes far away, and then the strengthening wind extinguished the mumbling voices completely.

Hence he thought it was a gang of smugglers from Bohemia who came over there clandestinely almost every night and, once over the border, deposited their heavily loaded packs for a short pause of breath. So he went back to sleep reassured, if not also sinking completely into dreaming, but only into a humming sleep, as it were, which befogged his brain and tore all sorts of half images past it.

In the first light of morning, he awoke again. And when he raised his head, he felt the echo of a weak knocking in his ear. He climbed out of bed, put his trousers on, went to the window to take a look at the weather and saw frosty tatters of mist blowing over a morose morning. For that reason, he threw another coat on and then climbed, somewhat grumbly and drowsy, carefully down the stairs.

Right after he opened the door, he almost stepped on a human hand. For a man was thrown down across the three steps in the pose of someone exhausted to death, whose strength had abandoned him, had probably arrived at the entrance of the inn with his last efforts and tried to reach for the door handle with his hand. He was wearing a greyish green sport coat, his head, from which the little felt hat had slid, was resting on a fully packed rucksack, and his slicker had been drawn cursorily over his body. From his long, white hands and gaunt, sharply sculptured head, his shoes and the fallen, horn pince-nez which lay on the dew-wet stone threshold next to his thin, slightly bent nose, the landlord recognised that it was a man of the better classes, perhaps an academic.

"Hey there!" he now called cautiously, bent down and shook the stranger gently on the shoulder. He did not stir. For that reason, the landlord said his "hey there!" still louder, even closer to the ears, shook him harder and shouted almost, "Where are you wanting to go? You can't stay lying here in the cold. What is it with you then, hey there? Listen. Hey! You are at the snow cirques' inn!" Then the man emitted a long, anguished groan, slowly raised up his upper body, shivered, stared with averted face for a long time into the mist, which was swirling from the cirque and being torn apart above by the wind, and then turned to the landlord such a sorrowful face, with such deeply set eyes that he did not look like a drowsy man, but more like a madman. And what he said also indicated to the landlord a loss of mind.

For after the stranger had looked at the good-natured man for a while penetratingly, as if he had to work his look through a layer of haze, he broke out into derisive, garish laughter.

"Be ashamed, man," he said with knitted brows, "be ashamed that you are a man! There you stand fat and solid, and sleeping in a warm bed, and down below all over the world, men are dying in blood. Raging like beasts. Betraying one another, turning the cities into rubbish heaps. Why don't you pack as many pieces of stone as you can gather, and roll them down, throw them all into the wreckage. For this world must perish. This order originates from hell. Don't you have the courage for extremities in your chest, for the anarchy of heaven which you carry within ...?"

The stranger spoke further in convulsions, with a hoarse, shouting voice.

Slowly the landlord stepped back from the weird man, away into the house, and hurried up the stairs to overpower the blatant lunatic with his son's help so that he did not fall into the abyss of the cirque in his delusion.

Running as fast as he could, he sprang up the two flights to below the roof, shook the boy, and shouted, "Up Gustav! Get up and dressed quick. There is a lunatic lying down below in front of the door." But it was a hard bit of work to get the sleeper to awake.

And when the two finally came down, the steps were empty and despite a long search and much calling, no trace was found of the strange, weird man.

Then they thought he must have plunged into the cirque.

But when it was all searched in the perfect light, nothing was discovered there either.

The landlord was questioned the next day by the commander of the border police who had rushed up. The watchfulness of the strengthened troops increased and after a few days, two soldiers standing on the plateau before the Spindler inn saw a tall, gaunt man going back and forth aimlessly through the mountain pines on the high Sturmhaube. They called to him to stay where he was and one even put his rifle to his cheek ready to fire. But when the sound of the call reached the man, he ducked and ran in long strides in all directions through the stunted trees, but always in the direction of the Austrian border. The soldiers ran up the mountain after him as hard as they could. But when they reached the place where he had just been among the pines, there was nothing to be seen or heard all around. Only, a wheatear rose up not far from them with its short shrill trilling into the primordial silence of the crest, and in the White Elbe valley it was simmering dreamily out of the darkness of the firs like soft rippling waves. Finally, a week later, a tourist thought she saw him. Her observations admittedly could only be fitted within the frame of the image of the "wild Professor" which the people had created over the course of days.

She came in the darkness of evening out of the valley of Mummel from Harachsdorf past the Wosseker inn and was stepping bravely on to reach the old Silesian inn before nightfall.

When she had reached the crest, she took a look back to Krkonoše, which lay in the haze of evening like an enormous crouching animal in a smoking meadow. While she was thus looking over the area from which she had come, a man's voice began singing "Deutschland, Deutschland über alles" in the direction of the gentle saddle towards the Reifträger. The singing sounded with cutting derison, broke off already after the first two lines of verse and merged into a garish derisive laughter. When she looked down the crest path, she caught sight of a tall, thin man, who stopped every moment between lusty strides and belted the stunted pines with furious blows of his stick as if they were his enemies.

Thus with singing, shrill laughter, halting and battling, he drove on for quite a while until he threw his hat, stick and rucksack aside and sank exhausted amongst the pines.

The woman was seized with horror and pity, and when, from the area where he had settled down, a few loud sobs and groans rung out, it stuck in the listener's throat and full of fear and angst, she ran down into the valley.

That was the last time Professor Weitfeld was seen in the mountains. Then he vanished from the area and from Silesia.

After the revolutionary, November collapse of Germany in the same year, he emerged in Berlin as the leader of that left wing of the independent

Social Democrats which became the Communists with the progress of the national break-up.

It is still in the memory of all who have followed those events attentively, what a pernicious role he played in the Berliners' struggles around the Silesian railway station, in the months of the blossoming of the Brunswick Communism and during the bloody soviet dictatorship in Munich.

His fanatical idealism was as pure and as criminal as that of Eisner and Landauer.

He also encountered a similar end to these men. With the struggle of the red army against the troops of the defence force intruding into Munich, the white guards, he fought in the vanguard of the communists who were defending themselves desperately at the Sendling gate against the superior powers. There he too found his death by a bullet and was buried in a mass grave.

About the Publisher

Our mission is to provide translations into English of the complete works of neglected major European writers. We do not cherry-pick works that seem the most marketable, but rather seek to provide a complete collection of each writer's works so that readers can follow the writer's development and decide on its merits for themselves.

http://www.facebook.com/KANitzPublishing